FRIENDS AND ENEMIES

Friends and Enemies

NAOMI
MITCHISON

ILLUSTRATED BY

Caroline Sassoon

The John Day Company, New York

First American Edition, 1968

Library of Congress Catalogue Card Number:
68-11185
PRINTED IN THE UNITED STATES OF AMERICA

Diteng

(Tse di mo teng)

Contents

Foreword

This book is about what really happens in a real town called Mochudi in Bechuanaland. The family in the story is invented, but there are lots of people like that in Mochudi. I am a Mokgatla myself so I know. Petrus and his brother are invented too, but there are real people to whom such things are happening now. But Chief Linchwe is real and so are several of the other people in the book. If you look carefully you will even find me in it. This year a lot of children like those in the book would have died but for the help Oxfam—Oxford Committee for Famine Relief—and War on Want have been giving.

The stories in the book are almost all taken from *Kgatla Animal Stories* collected by Lestrade and Schapera. Some were told by people I know. Professor Schapera lived among the Bakgatla for quite a long time and has written many books and papers about them and the rest of the Batswana.

FRIENDS AND ENEMIES

IMPORTANT PEOPLE IN THIS BOOK

Kgosi Linchwe II, *Paramount Chief of the Bakgatla. He is also called* Kgabo *because this is the Word of the Tribe.* Kgabo *means either monkey or flame of fire, and is used in greeting or to the Chief.*

Letsebe, *his sister* Dineo, *and his brother-cousin* Pheto, *and their little brothers and sisters*

Their father Molemi *and their mother* Tsholofelo

Their grannie Nkoko

Petrus Mangope *and his elder brother* Joseph, *his mother and his little brother and sister*

Mr. Phirie, *Educational Secretary of the Bakgatla*

The people of Bechuanaland call themselves the Batswana; *one man or woman is a* Motswana. *The people of my own tribe, the* Kgatla, *call themselves the* Bakgatla; *one man or woman is a* Mokgatla, *and the thirty thousand square miles of land where they live is called the* Kgatleng. *Soon after the action in this book took place, Bechuanaland became* Botswana, *the place of the* Tswara *people.*

CHAPTER 1

At the Cattle Post

WAS IT EVER GOING TO RAIN? How thin the poor cows looked, the ones that were left! There was the young, delicately spotted cow with the even curve to her horns; she had calved but she had so little milk for the new calf. Letsebe stood and watched them, frowning like a man. There was not enough milk for him to take any; the poor knobbly, bony calf must have it all if it was to live. So many of the cattle had died.

There was no grass left. When he and the others drove out the cattle they had to go farther and farther, looking for grazing. Letsebe rode the ox he had tamed himself, but it had no spirit, just plodded on, snatching at a bush now and then, a dry bush.

The ground around the borehole was all chawed up by the impatient hoofs of the beasts shouldering one another aside to get at the troughs. Would the borehole hold out? Letsebe watched and listened to the men talking. He could not understand quite where this water came from, away under the ground, cool and dark, with a different taste from rain water or river water. Perhaps if he went to school he would understand.

He sat on the ground, waiting for the cattle to finish drinking. It was hot and dusty and he had carried the new calf part of the way, with its mother pushing him and smelling at it over his shoulder. He wore a belt with a little leather flap on it, but the older boys and men mostly had shorts, torn and patched most likely, but the dress of grown people, Christians. He too was a Christian; and he could sing many hymns, harmonizing them until they sounded well. He too could frighten his younger sisters with stories of hellfire, worse than the stories of old war which his grandfather used to tell before he became ill and went to the Mission hospital and died.

Someone had shot a buck and now it was skinned and hanging on a tree, not nice without its brown fur, but very nice when it was cooked over the fire. It was a big buck, bigger than a goat, but not so good to eat; nothing is better than a young, fat goat. He measured the

16

cooked meat with his eyes; there would surely be a bit
for him when his father and the rest had eaten, not a
very tender part, but perhaps something with a bone he
could chew for a long time. There would be sour milk in
the bag that had been hung up on another branch, but
no porridge to eat with it. There was no woman here to
do the cooking. Mother was at home, at Mochudi, a
long day's walk from the cattle post.

The sun was dropping now, the heat beginning to
drain out of the brown dust and the brittle gray-green
leaves. The heat ate up one's strength. If only he could

jump into a river and swim, get cool all over! "I wish there was a river here beside my feet!" he said to his cousin Pheto.

"What would you do?" said Pheto. He too was chewing at a piece of bone and tendon.

"I would swim. I would be wet all over. My toes would swim. There would be no dust on me anywhere."

"Do you remember the last time we swam?" said Pheto, and he giggled, his eyes screwing up into the laughter behind them.

"There is nothing to remember!" said Letsebe crossly.

"I remember very well that you had a talk with Kgosi's whip."

"That I cannot remember," said Letsebe, and threw a stone at a lizard.

"It would be a harder talk the next time," said Pheto. "Kgosi said we were not to swim in the river because of this illness that lives in the mud. The illness with the long name."

"I remember the name," said Letsebe, "I almost remember!" His face grew heavy with trying to remember the name. "It is bilharzia. That was what the Chief said."

"What his whip said," Pheto remarked.

"He told us he had it once himself because he too swam and was not enough beaten for it, and that the

18

cure takes long and is worse than many whips. But is this true or does the illness come because some enemy has put it upon one?"

Letsebe and Pheto were whispering now. It was beginning to be dark, though there was a glow still in the air above them and the sky streaked with orange gold. But the come-to-supper star was bright and big and the other stars beginning to show, high and high. You could hear the cattle moving all the time before they settled for the night, the muffled tinkle of bells, and behind the sounds of the cattle the sudden calls and honking of the evening birds.

"The old people say it comes from an enemy," Pheto said, "our fathers and their fathers. Surely they must be wise?"

"But if *he* says otherwise? The Chief has been far away, flying up in the sky. He was sent to get knowledge. We were left without him so that he could learn. We must believe him."

"Yes," said Pheto, "we must believe Kgosi."

They were tired. It had been a long day out with the cattle. If they had been well fed, they would have played, wrestled, run races, taught tricks to the oxen. But if you were hungry you did not play. You watched and slept and thought about rain.

There was a fire of sticks which some of them had brought in. There were sticks put in starwise, so that the broken ends burned and you could always push them farther into the fire. Letsebe could see the shape of the head and shoulders of his father Molemi between him and the fire. His father on whom it depended whether he too was to get knowledge: not so much knowledge as the Chief, but some knowledge. To know what writing says. To count, not just with one's fingers. To wear a shirt and shorts. To go to school.

He knew his father and mother had spoken of it, and perhaps his uncles. There was also his cousin Nkomeng, who was a big girl in the secondary school. She was going to get her diploma, then perhaps teach or work in an office wearing shoes and a white blouse clean every day. And now, because of this education, she was able to join in talk with her elders as though she were a grown woman—almost as though she were a man! She wanted everyone to go to school and get knowledge. His uncle had spent much money on this education that Nkomeng was having. The first year's education cost only fifty cents a year, but later it got more and more expensive. So many books! So many teachers! Nkomeng went to their own secondary school. If she had gone to one of the big Mission schools, that would have cost even more. Their uncle was richer than they were; he had been lucky with his cattle and he had only three children. But he was not as rich as that. As it was, it cost him an ox a year to keep Nkomeng at school. A whole ox!

But if Letsebe was to go to school, it must be soon. He knew that after a boy was eleven years old he could not begin to go to the school. It was a rule, a law. In the old days boys and girls started when they were older, when they were young men and women, big and strong, and if they disobeyed the teacher, what could he do? They were too big for the teacher to beat. So now it was said that no child over ten could be enrolled. And Letsebe was nearly eleven; this year was his only chance.

His cousin Pheto was the same age. They were almost brothers. Pheto's father, who had been killed by a truck, had been Molemi's younger brother, so it was right and natural that Pheto and his brother and sister and his mother should come to live with them. Then there had been another woman's hands to pound the meal and sweep out the lapa. But Pheto's mother, too, had died, and Tsholofelo, Letsebe's mother, had been all the kinder to them, although it meant that she must do all the pounding. But the name Tsholofelo means Hope, and she had always been hopeful; she had always thought that things were really all right and better times would surely come. She had not minded that she had so much more work to do. Soon the two girls would be old enough to help a great deal. For there was Dineo, who was nine years old and could pound the full of a corn mortar before she got so tired that she could not lift the beater. Pheto's sister Dikeledi was only seven years old and she could not pound yet. But she could sweep with a little whisk, and besides she was good at looking after the little ones. Her name was Dikeledi, which means tears. That was because another child had died just before she was born.

The men went on talking in low voices and sometimes one of them would tell the tail end of a story or say something which brought a story or saying to mind. Then there was sometimes a little laughter. They spoke of the illnesses of cattle. And always, always, the talk came back to the rain. What had happened to the rain? Why was there no rain? How could the rain be made to come? *Pula, pula.* That is the word for rain. If there is no rain there is no food. Nothing to eat. It is as simple as that.

All the sunset had faded out of the sky. The enormous arch of stars turned slowly above them. A spark or two trailed out of the fire as someone pushed in a stick. The head-high dark branches, close set and strong, stood firm against any danger to them or their cattle. Now a noise came out of the night, the noise of a wild beast hunting. It ranged round, but the men felt safe, knew they were safe. From everything but hunger. Some of them had rifles with them. But cartridges had to be bought. And where was money to come from? If rain, good crops, enough to sell, even. If rain, good grass for the beasts, fat oxen to sell. Money. So it went around.

But if there was rain now, tonight, if the ground was soaked with good rain, people would still not be able to plow. The plow oxen were so weak and thin they could barely walk as far as the grazing grounds. They would have to eat to grow strong, before they could be yoked to the plow. That is, you could do nothing on the lands until after the second rains. The first rain would bring the grass. The plow oxen would eat it and be strengthened. Then you could yoke them to the carts and carry the plows out to the lands; at the second rain you would plow.

A few rich men had tractors or could afford to hire them from those that had them. They could plow after the first rains and some of them did, but sometimes they too waited till their neighbors were plowing. People's ideas do not always keep pace with their machines.

The boys were asleep now, curled in the still warm dust, dusty themselves. One by one the men spread their blankets and went to sleep. The waning moon rose late, blotting out the stars around it, showing up the dark points of the enclosing and sheltering stockade around the cattle kraal.

These were men and boys of the Kgatla, one of the eight tribes of the Bechuanaland Protectorate. But part of the tribe was in Bechuanaland and part was across the border in the Republic of South Africa. The boundary line between the two countries had been drawn by strangers far away, some of them in London, who did not know about the Bakgatla and they had been drawn along what seemed obvious lines, for instance, a big river. But the same people, speaking the same language, friends and cousins, may easily live on the two sides of a river. People move or are driven away by their enemies. They look for new pastures for their cattle. In good years a tribe spreads out. But the people who drew the boundaries were white people; they did not bother with the black people whose lives might be altered by what they did. But if things became different at the two sides of a boundary line?

Sometimes people went across from Bechuanaland into the Republic of South Africa; there is more money there. You can earn enough to buy a cow, even two cows; the next year the cows may have calves. Then already you have enough to give as a present to the family of the girl you want to marry. Or, if you are married already, you can buy things to put in your house. You can buy dresses for your wife, or scent. Or you can buy yourself a plow or harrows or ox chains. One of the men had been away working at the mines in Johannesburg for two years; the pay there was much better than pay at white farms, but it was harder work. Some men spent all the money they had earned, but he had kept his. He had earned enough to bring back many presents and to buy two cows in calf. This way he had become a cattle owner and now had a share at the borehole cattle post. It was important not to have too many cattle at any one borehole. If there was overgrazing all the grass got trodden out and would not recover; then the soil begins to blow away and cracks, and erosion starts. That is perhaps how some of the world's deserts were made.

The land where the borehole was belonged to the tribe, to the Bakgatla. In the geography books it is called a tribal reserve to show that other people cannot walk in and take a bit. The men called it the Kgatleng and although it was so bare and harsh and poor they loved it, and if they left it for a while they were always deeply glad to come back to it. When they saw the shape of the low granite hills of the Kgatleng rising above the horizon, their hearts were full of thanks. Once more they were home.

When land belongs to a Tribe, one person cannot own a bit of it. The idea of doing that seems crazy to many Africans. You cannot own the land where the grass grows any more than you can own the air you breathe or the running waters of a river. But if anyone wants to plow and take a crop on a particular piece of land, or to build a house somewhere, then he must get leave from the Tribe. That is, in practice, from the Chief. Because the Tribe makes and belongs to the Chief, just as the Chief makes and belongs to the Tribe. A good Chief will not refuse any reasonable thing that is asked of him by one of his tribesmen, or indeed by others. A Chief should be always a giver.

And the Bakgatla knew they had a good Chief.

CHAPTER 2

In the Location

SIXTY MILES AWAY, only sixty miles, and everything was different. People didn't sleep on the ground, they didn't hear wild beasts in the night. They wore proper clothes all the time. Even little boys and girls wore clothes, lest their parents should be shamed. They had houses with windows and chimneys. For this was no longer Bechuanaland, though the people were Batswana. When they thought of themselves that way. But that was not how they thought of themselves, mostly. It would have been too proud a way.

The Mangope family had a three-roomed house with a stoep, a little veranda up two steps, and on it a few bright flowers planted in old gasoline cans which had

26

been painted red and green, and even a clump of canna lilies beside the steps. The corrugated iron roof kept off the rain and caught it in a water butt when it came, though this roof was not as warm as the thatch which Mrs. Mangope remembered from her childhood. The three small windows were polished clean; only one pane was cracked.

Inside there was a round table with enough chairs or stools for the family, framed wedding photographs on the walls, curtains at the windows. In one room was a big bed for Mrs. Mangope and the two younger children, with a high, battered chest of drawers, filled to bursting with clothes and bits of clothes which might one day come in handy, worn shoes, bits of toys, things bought at jumble sales. In the other room there were two hard couches for Petrus and his big brother Joseph, the teacher and earner for the family. There was a polished brass lamp and some ornaments in plastic, a comic cat and a vase full of paper flowers. And over Joseph's couch and the neatly folded blanket, a shelf with a few school textbooks and a Bible in Afrikaans. There was a small battery radio set that sometimes worked. All these things, all this comfort! But this was the Republic of South Africa.

There were three or four other books, not school-books and not with Joseph's name in them, and they were hidden in the chest of drawers, under the worn

27

clothes. For books can be dangerous. Words can be dangerous. Ideas can be dangerous. Out of books Joseph and some of his friends had got the idea that black men were as good as white, that they had just as much right to be educated, to become doctors and lawyers and professors, to make laws for everybody, to own land and all that could be done with land, to have a share in the wealth of a country full of gold and diamonds and prosperity.

But it was dangerous to have these ideas. Mrs. Mangope knew it and would not touch the books, only buried them deeper, in case a policeman should march in and look for them. It was safer to be the way she was, to sweep and clean and sew, to look at the shopwindows with the electric light in them, glittering over new, bright things, but not to want these things too much: to look at the posters on the outside of the cinema, but not even to want to go in and see these wonderful things which were only for the baases and their ladies. It was better to go to church among one's fellows and sing hymns, one after another, and not to think, as Joseph thought, that God would rather see black and white people sitting next to one another in one congregation. Why did her son Joseph have to think? Was it because he was a teacher? But not all teachers did this thinking. The other teacher in Joseph's school did not want to think. Some teachers just went to the school every day and made the children repeat arithmetic tables and lists of spellings. And they drew the same pay as Joseph. So why did he have to think?

Yet sometimes, when Joseph and his friends were talking, she couldn't help listening and then everything seemed to grow bigger and more shining. There was a place for pride. It was not always to be a land of white master and black servant. That would come to an end. But Mrs. Mangope never listened for long and she tried not to let Petrus listen. She sent him to the tap at the corner of the street for a bucket of water. She sent him off to collect wood for the kitchen fire, or with ten cents to buy a small piece of meat, or a little rice or meal, or a box of matches, even sometimes a can of sausage meat or beans. Yes, and he could get a pennyworth of sweets for himself and the little ones. Yes, if he stayed away from the dangerous talk.

But, more and more, Petrus didn't want to stay away when the others came and sat around the table and talked. He began to understand that once there had been something called a political party. People talked about it, using letters only. But now it was no longer allowed. There could not be a meeting; there could not be a thing called a trade union. Once, when three others were there, a loud knock came on the locked door. Joseph hurried to open it, calling yes, yes, and one of the others quickly spread a pack of cards on the table, so that it looked like a game. But it was only a woman knocking, a neighbor who had come to ask Mrs. Mangope to help with a sick baby. Not the police.

It was nicest when Joseph talked to Petrus alone. Petrus was at the school where his big brother taught. It was from Joseph's salary that Petrus got his school fees. They were only a few shillings, but many fathers and mothers did not want to pay for sending a child to school, or did not have the money. And it was from Joseph's salary that they got the food they ate, the rent they paid for their house and the taxes they had to pay on the top of that. Their father had worked hard and done without drink and betting or anything that made life more fun, to pay for his eldest son to be trained as a teacher. And then one hard winter he had begun to cough very much and a time came when they took him away to the hospital and he never came back. But by then Joseph was earning.

A day came when Joseph was staying late at the school to write out the next week's syllabus of lessons neatly, in between ruled lines. He and the other master had to see that the school was clean and tidy, ready for the next day. The bigger girls were supposed to do this, but often they rushed off, leaving it half done. The other teacher was an oldish man, surly, who often punished the children. Joseph hated punishing them. He liked practicing games with them; he himself was a good sprinter. The school had no playground, but on a Saturday they would all go off to a bit of level ground where they had cleared the bushes, and play soccer. The boys had saved, cent by cent, to buy the ball and some even had boots. Joseph had learned the proper rules out of a book. The boys were good with their feet, clever with the ball, but often they forgot the rules.

He taught them jumping too. They had made a sand pit for the long jump and poles for the high jump. There was one boy who was very good. But now, at school, Joseph was thinking about him and something that had happened, and he began to worry. He worried so much that he could not make the lines straight. He had to stop and put his head down on the ink-smelling table, trying to think it out. His hair was cut very short, so that it was in little tight curls all over his head, like a decoration on a dark bronze head. Against this darkness of his head and throat his shirt, which his mother washed and ironed and carefully darned, was very white. The fingers gripping now at his forehead were fine and narrow.

This boy he was thinking about was called David. He was a big, smiling boy, long-legged. On a good day he could jump well, going up from four feet to five, coming in cleverly, flinging both legs up, careful to keep clear. And Joseph kept thinking, It might be a way out for him, if he can be good enough, it is something that even *they* respect a little. Yes, if David keeps on, he may become a champion, proud, free—he might even go overseas! But he did not dare say this yet, he could only urge David on, reading from his little book the faults a jumper might have and trying to see them in David and correct them if need be.

The boys were running barefoot, their shirts carefully piled in case they tore them. First they had practiced and now they were jumping against one another, and some of the bigger girls, who were watching them, were cheering them on. David seemed to wince as he ran, but he jumped beautifully. Only when he landed, he swore under his breath, a bad swear. Joseph frowned and went to him. But then he saw that the boy had a thorn in his foot, one of the bad, three-pronged burs that go through even the tough skins of those used to walking barefoot. So he said nothing about the swear, but helped to get it out.

"It was on the run-in," said David, "but I made my jump, Teacher."

"You were like one of Chaka's warriors," said Joseph, and then suddenly he found himself telling the boys and girls how Chaka, the Zulu king, had trained his soldiers to run silently, never stopping, not burdened with oxhide sandals, and he had done this by making them dance barefoot to the sound of drums and singing on ground strewn with thorns like this thorn—and he held it up—until they were the bravest in the world. And Joseph had looked around with thoughts of courage in his heart and had seen it come back at him through the eyes of his pupils. And suddenly he knew that what he was offering them was dangerous, as dangerous as strong drink.

Then one of the boys had made the correct school response which they had learned: "But Chaka was a tyrant, Chaka was cruel—"

And Joseph had said yes, but he had not said it properly, for in his heart he knew that Chaka was a hero, although he had killed. And this other boy, Sampson, had watched him, and now Joseph wondered. It was well known that boys at school were told to watch their teachers, in case— They were paid for doing that, paid whole shillings. Well, thought Joseph, I will be careful, I will be most careful, I will only teach in school according to the syllabus. I will teach that Retief and his men were Christian and noble and that Dingaan was a treacherous savage. But one day, one day— And in his heart he was hating the history syllabus and Bantu Education.

But what use is it to hate a history syllabus if it is one's living and the living of one's family? It brought food and shelter. It brought education for Petrus and later for Rebecca and the little Luke. And education was part of the way out. If only it could go on! But at the very best it seemed only to lead to the Bantu colleges and that was not a way out. Not a way to the great world beyond the Republic of South Africa where, so they said, it did not matter what color your skin was. The great world where an African might become the most learned of scientists in a laboratory, respected by white scientists who would not even think of him as black—but was that possible? Joseph did not know what was possible and what was dreams, but he had seen pictures, he had read letters which were passed from hand to hand. He made a little groaning noise and dusted the chalk off his hands and hair, stood up, put the chair neatly in place for his next day, saw that the windows were shut and the door locked, and walked back through the location to his own house.

This part of the town was all African. The whites lived in an altogether different part. They had big houses in gardens with proper fences between them. There was enough water for baths. Some even had electricity. If only they could have had that in the school! The white ladies did not work; African women came and worked for them, scrubbing and washing. Sometimes the white girls worked as clerks and cashiers; they were very proud and you must be extra careful if you spoke to them, if, for example, you needed jotters or pencils for the school. These girls made more money than a head teacher, though sometimes they did not add up the change right. But you must not say so.

The African part of the town, the location, had no streetlights; the houses were crowded and some of them were badly built and untidy; the children were dirty and played in the gutter. A drunk man was shouting; a woman screamed. The big boys who did not go to school because their parents had no money or laughed at schooling went about in gangs and sometimes set on decent people like the Mangopes. So Joseph hurried; for it was beginning to get dark.

His mother had waited with the cooking and she had become anxious. So many things might have happened! When he came to the stoep she hurried to the door with the frying pan in her hand, the hot fat smoking in it. But when she saw there was nothing wrong she spoke sharply and went back to the kitchen. Petrus was learning lists of words with difficult spellings, Afrikaans words. But he knew English, too. This was taught at the school in the top classes only, but Joseph had already made his brother learn, had made him read English aloud. But what was there to read from? Some of these books with the ideas in them. Even a storybook in English told about another world.

The lamp was lighted and put in the middle of the table on a square of cloth that Mrs. Mangope had embroidered in cross-stitch a long time ago, when she herself had been for a time at a kind of school that taught housework, so that afterwards she had become a house-girl getting good wages. Her Madam had often praised her and given her things. She still had some of the skirts and blouses, kept for best, although they were thirty years old.

She sat at one side of the table, Joseph at the other, Petrus between his mother and Joseph, Rebecca and Luke at the far side. Rebecca would be coming to school next year. Already she knew some of her letters. She had a big pink bow pinned on her dress and ducked and giggled as Joseph cupped her head in his hands. None of the children wore shoes or stockings; their toes were free to wriggle. And Joseph had taken off his own shoes and socks that he wore all the time when he was being a teacher. They had tea with sugar and condensed milk and mealie pap with some meat gravy to go with it, but the bits of meat went to Joseph. He was the one who had earned them. Then they had syrup balls.

The plates were a mixed lot. Rebecca had the one with the flowers on it. The tea mugs were pink-and-blue plastic, new. Joseph had given them to his mother out of his last quarter's salary; they looked pretty in the lamplight. Joseph said the grace. The others had their eyes shut and did not see a kind of misery on Joseph, who wondered how long God, to whom he was speaking, would allow certain things to go on. Things that didn't make sense.

In the Location

After the little ones were in bed, Mrs. Mangope went over to see a neighbor; her man was in jail and she was having a poor time. Mrs. Mangope had kept back two syrup balls to take for her children. Petrus went over his word list again. The arithmetic tables he knew. He looked up and there was his brother watching him from across the lamp. They were rather alike, with their long-fringed dark eyes and straight, delicate noses over full, kindly mouths.

"You heard what I said to David?" said Joseph abruptly.

"Yes," said Petrus, "there was plenty of speaking about it. Sampson, he said Teacher praised Chaka."

"I wish that Sampson was at the bottom of a well," said Joseph somberly.

"But you said nothing wrong!" said Petrus. Suddenly he was anxious.

"There are those that think it wrong—to say anything good—about ourselves. Forget it, Petrus. Perhaps Sampson too will forget it."

For a minute Petrus went back to his spellings. Then he said, "Joseph. We aren't Zulus, us?"

"No, Petrus, we can't speak in clicks. Not like Xhosa people. But our own people were brave too. Our father was half Pedi, our mother pure Motswana. Like people in Bechuanaland."

"In Bechuanaland? But, Joseph, those people are savages."

"They are poor. They were driven into poor country when the others came."

"The others? The brave voortrekkers?" Pictures jumped into his mind out of his history books: voortrekkers in their laagers, firing, with the savages around them howling and brandishing spears.

"So it says in the book," Joseph said.

And suddenly Petrus felt himself shaken by the tone in his brother's voice. "But—if they were savages—not Christian—"

"They did not have guns. Is that being a savage? They are still poor, they live in harsh, dry country. But we have cousins there. One day, perhaps, we will go

38

there, Petrus, you and I. I would like to know how it feels to be free."

"Free?"

"No white baas. To live one's own life. Under one's own laws. Even poor."

"One's own laws," said Petrus waveringly.

"Petrus," said Joseph, leaning over the table, "you have heard me talk with my friends sometimes. You must have listened."

"I know not to speak," said Petrus solemnly.

"You have heard us speak of other countries in Africa, where Africans, black people like ourselves, rule one another. Where we make our own laws. Do you believe we speak true?"

"Seems queer," said Petrus at last, picking with his nail at the edge of the table. "Not easy to believe, that. This country—Ghana—"

"Ghana. Nigeria. Kenya. Tanzania. Malawi that is just north of us, Zambia—you remember who makes laws in that Zambia?"

Petrus made an effort, then got it. "Kaunda. Kenneth Kaunda. But—he is truly—African—like ourselves?"

"Truly."

"I can't somehow understand," said Petrus.

"You will," said Joseph, "and listen, my brother. If that Sampson says any more, you tell me. Tell me quick. Could be dangerous. If the police hear—"

"I understand," said Petrus, and then, "The song.

Even that. You told me. If the police were to know—"

"Yes," said Joseph and very low began to hum the song "God Save Africa." And, very low, Petrus joined in.

CHAPTER 3

At Mochudi

"TODAY WE GO TO MOCHUDI," said Letsebe's father Molemi, softly and suddenly. It was barely light, the eastern sky barred with orange. All around them small birds were singing and twittering; later the hot strike of the sun would quiet them. Little blue-gray doves cooed and rustled. "I have things to speak about to your mother," he went on, as Letsebe rolled over and onto his feet. "Wrap this piece of cooked meat in leaves. Find a can, we will take some milk. And you, Letsebe, drink before we start, it is far enough."

Pheto was awake now. "Do I come, our father?"

"No," said Molemi, "you will herd the cattle. Take

41

care of the new calf; carry her if she is tired. And do not drink one drop of her milk. Obey your uncle Thotwe."

"I hear, Father," said Pheto obediently, but disappointed. Thotwe was Molemi's elder brother, the lucky uncle. The name Thotwe means the bundle you carry; it had been a lucky bundle! But Letsebe was disappointed too that his brother-cousin was not coming with them. The way would have been shorter with Pheto; he could not joke with his father or ask him riddles.

Molemi said little as they walked. He was thinking. Sometimes he looked at the sky, in case a cloud might have come sailing up. But none came all that morning. There were tracks through the bush; you could see where cattle had been and where people, where the delicate threading of an impala had dented the sand, or the heavier hoof marks of wildebeest or koodoo. Molemi noticed them all and sometimes spoke of them to Letsebe. There were snake spoors where the big snakes had pushed their wriggling way through the sand. Here a hyena had crossed, but well back into the night that was over. There were two jackals running. Once Molemi stopped and laughed because he had seen the track of a friend of his who had lost the top joint of his big toe, so that it was plain to read and he was hurrying, why? Molemi would certainly find out. Rapula was in his own *mophato,* his regiment. And this footprint was scarcely an hour old. If a man is in your own regiment, he will not have secrets from you. It is almost as if he is your brother.

Letsebe kept a watch for berries or anything to eat, but everything was so dried up, the bushes seemed to be all spikes. Only the insects constantly ran and jumped and danced over twigs and stones and dry leaves. The throats of the little lizards throbbed and their eyes looked warily around. Letsebe got more and more thirsty. The long drink he had taken before starting had all sweated out of him.

After a while his father stopped, looked for a stick, sharpened it with his knife and dug in the ground below a tuft of leaves. He pulled out two or three thick roots and took off the outer skin. Letsebe was pleased; he held out his hands for one of them; they did not taste of anything very much, but as you bit into them, you almost got a full drink of water. They were not as nice as watermelons, but how many months till there would be watermelons again! The seeds were not even sown, could not be until after the rains.

They went on, less thirsty; now they were walking along a definite track with wheel marks. And it began to seem to Molemi that the clouds were coming up a little, that there seemed to be some promise. Oh rain, rain. The track became more definite, sometimes through bush, sometimes with high, shady trees at each side.

The tree roots went down deep, sucking up water that was out of reach of the crop plants. From time to time they saw cattle and spoke of them. Letsebe was slowly learning what a beautiful cow should be like and how some kinds of marking and some shapes of head or horns went together in harmony. But how thin they all were! Many cows had died already that year. They met some friends and stopped for greetings and courtesies and to speak of the signs or not-signs of rain coming. It was said that there had been good rains a hundred miles to the north. Was that true? How had it come about?

Now they were out of the bush and among the lands, walking between hedges of cut thorn bush. But nobody was plowing yet. Nobody was living in their houses on the lands. No use till the rain came.

They were meeting more people now; some of them were looking sadly at their lands or at the sky. There was a low crackle of thunder, but far off, no use. They were near Mochudi now and Letsebe felt he could not walk another mile. When his father stopped to speak to friends, he flopped down at the side of the path.

But at least they were among houses. Soon, soon, they would be home. No more walking. A long, long drink of water. This was their town, their dear Mochudi.

There are nearly twenty thousand people living in Mochudi, or rather coming and going but with a house there. It is the center of the Kgatleng, the capital of the

Bakgatla. Here is the Tribal Office and the great kraal. Here above all is the Chief and the Chief's *kgotla*, the court of justice and meeting place for discussion and decision.

Some of the houses in Mochudi are round and are set on a circular platform with the eaves of the house coming down over it so that there is always somewhere one can sit out of the sun most of the year, but in its warmth during the three cold months. Some houses are square so that they can easily be divided up inside with a curtain, and here the front thatch comes down over a wide porch where things can be kept and where it is pleasant to work. That was the kind of house Molemi had built and Tsholofelo had plastered with cow dung and earth over walls and floor. Richer people built houses of brick and lime plaster with little pillars and colored concrete floors and roofs of shining corrugated iron, which is good for catching the rain; such houses always have big water butts standing beside them. They have newly built earth-closet shelters; for people know that these are civilized and healthy. Many people would like to build them if they had the money to pay for them.

But almost all houses, big houses and round rondavels alike, stand in a *lapa,* a courtyard plastered with the women's mixture of earth and cow dung, fresh and pleasant to walk on barefoot. However untidy it is outside, with old cans and strips of hide and bits of cardboard and prickly bushes, inside the lapa it is always swept out and clean. Around the lapa is a low wall, sometimes worked into steps, and at each side of the narrow doors into it and sometimes all around there are patterns drawn freehand by the women of the house, often the older ones, in gray and white or sometimes in red. Between the lapas there are rocks and bushes and cattle kraals with man-height palings

46

around them of gray branches set thickly together; these usually belong to the Ward, that is to say, to the division of Mochudi which started originally from one family, but may now be a thousand families. These kraals are needed for the oxen that pull the wagons and sleds, or the milk cows. But there are not so many of them. Most people in Mochudi, just like Molemi, have their cattle out at the cattle posts; if they want milk they get it from one of the goats. Mochudi is full of goats and pigs and dogs and straggly hens and some sheep. But above all Mochudi is full of trees, beautiful shade trees, set here and there, many different kinds, most of them planted by one man or another, and the roads and paths winding under and between them. Now Molemi and Letsebe turned onto one of them, and it was the way home.

Molemi was a Mokgatla, a man of the Kgatla tribe. And this meant a great deal. It meant duties and responsibilities toward others, above all toward the men of his own mophato and toward his Chief. But it also meant the good that one got from being a tribesman, the help one could count on from others. There are eight tribes in Bechuanaland, and the Bakgatla are not the biggest but they have a great record of education and progress. They are proud of plenty of things and schooling is one of them. The Tribe has built its own schools, under the direction and with the help of their Chiefs. Linchwe the First, the Chief who became a Christian, taking it all very seriously, started this; others have followed. The Chiefs were rich and proud then; they kept all the stray cattle for themselves; their fields were cultivated for them by the tribesmen; they could order out the regiments, that is to say the initiation groups, to do anything that had to be done. And nobody would have disobeyed them. In the old days the regiments fought for their Chief; now they do more useful things. This was the way the first schools got built.

Now the Chief is another Linchwe, still young, but already beginning to prove himself to the Tribe and to the whole country. He is just as keen on education as his ancestors were. He himself went overseas to England to finish his own education and while he was there he visited schools and asked questions and took notes, so that when the time came he could help his people as well as possible. But he no longer gets his lands cultivated free; he gets no stray cattle; and, though he can ask people to work for the community, and often they will do it because he has persuaded them and they think it is a good thing, yet he cannot force them to, even when it is for the general good. They are his people; he can and should lead them. If they follow, good and well. But sometimes they don't want to follow; these are the people who are lazy or stupid, or feel he is going too fast.

48

Molemi was one of those who sometimes felt the Chief was going too fast. For a long time, before there were all these schools and all this talk of progress, it had been the custom for the girls to help their mothers at home and the boys to go out herding the cattle. Molemi had herded his father's cattle and had not gone to school till he was fourteen. And look, he could read and write! Not very well, because he had only got to Standard IV. After that his father had thought it was a waste of time; besides he hadn't had the money for the school fees and the clean shirt that should be worn. Only a few shillings, but if it isn't there, what then? His wife Tsholofelo, his children's mother, had only got to Standard II, but she very seldom needed to read; she was too busy.

Letsebe had dropped behind, so that his father and mother could greet one another, but his sister Dineo leaned over the wall of the lapa and waved at him. Then she lifted up her little sister, Mosidi, so that she could see over the wall, and Mosidi waved and laughed.

Most Tswana people's names mean something. It may be quite an elaborate phrase, or it may mean a nickname. Parents are usually known by the name of their eldest child, so Letsebe's father, Molemi, would usually be called Rraletsebe and his mother Mmaletsebe. But Molemi, who was very fond of his wife, for whom he had worked so hard, getting together the cattle for her family before they could be married,

49

building her a house and working for her, called her by her own name from their courting days, Tsholofelo—Hope. When he spoke her name, hope came back to him. His own name, Molemi, means plowman. Many people have that name.

And now Letsebe was drinking from a water jug that had been kept in the shade and was at least cool; down and down went the water, bringing him alive again, his arms and legs, his fingers and toes. Dineo brought a damp cloth and he rubbed himself all over, getting rid of the dust. It was only after this that he began to feel hungry. Dineo brought him a bowl half full of cold millet porridge, sour tasting and solid and good; he dug his fingers into it. There was a little goat's milk in a can to go with it, but that is not as good as cow's milk. "Dineo," he said, "what are they speaking about?"

"They are speaking about our school," said Dineo. Her name, Dineo, means gifts. Her father and mother had been happy to have a girl child. Like most of the children she had a Mission name as well. Hers was Rachel, but nobody used it. But if she went to the school, she would certainly tell it to the teacher. School!

"*Our* school?" said Letsebe. "Do you think you are going to school?"

"Today a girl must go to school," said Dineo, "so that she is as clever as the boys. More clever!"

"You could wait another year. You are only my younger sister."

"Why should I wait just because you are older than me? I know some of the letters already. I know English words—shil-ling—te-rain."

"You will have to wear real clothes at school—*if* you go there," said Letsebe, looking at his sister's string kilt which came down halfway to her knees in front, but left her behind bare.

"I shall have a gym tunic," said Dineo. "I shall look smart. Everyone will know I am going to school."

"And where will the money come from for that gym tunic?" said Letsebe. "Do you think Father will sell a cow to buy you a gym tunic!"

But that was indeed what Molemi and Tsholofelo were talking about in the dark inside of the house. Before going there, Molemi had gone to greet his mother, who lived in a separate round thatched house inside the same lapa. She was old, too old to help much with pounding the grain, though she could sit and sieve the meal and attend to the brewing when they had enough corn to make a potful of beer. After her son had spoken to her respectfully, giving her all the news, such as it was, he went back into his own house. Inside it was fairly cool and there was the nice smell of the reed thatch. They were talking about their children and this school. How could the money be found? "What shall we do, Tsholo?" Molemi said to his wife, shortening to the pet name.

"We will count the money," she said.

They sat down on the mud-plaster floor of their house, her bare feet sticking out under her blue skirt, his feet in broken ox-hide sandals. They looked into the can: there were many, many pennies, but not so much silver and still fewer rand, or two-rand notes. It was not only the school fees—though that would be hard enough. Letsebe and Pheto had each a pair of tattered shorts but not good enough for school; Pheto had a shrunken jersey but neither of them had a shirt. Dineo had only her kilt and a faded, pinkish, much-darned dress for Sundays. It would come to more money than the school fees if they were to be dressed decently so that they would not be laughed at. For a moment, Tsholofelo had the thought that perhaps Pheto need not go to school, but that was a wrong thought to have. His father had been her husband's younger brother; they must care for him always as their son.

Tsholofelo put aside the money that would be needed for the three at school. She had made up her mind that Dineo would go, even though she was so useful in the house, pounding the steeped grain, whisking the dust off the floor and the two chairs and the tin boxes, shaking the blankets and scouring the wooden porridge bowls with wood ash. Sometimes she polished the little lamp and dusted around the colored photograph of Molemi and Tsholofelo at their wedding, looking rather stiff and uncomfortable, but the only picture in the house. Yes, she would miss Dineo, though of course she could do a lot of work in the house after she came back from school every day. But when they were out on the lands? Anyhow, Dineo must go to school. But she did not tell her husband all that she thought, and she did not quite know why she so much wanted this schooling for Dineo, only that things must somehow be different for her daughter.

The school fee of fifty cents could be managed, though it would be more if the children stayed on into higher standards. To start with, the books and pencils came to another fifty-four cents. But clothes? She added another rand from the pile of grubby notes. Shoes or sandals could wait. If ever they got to secondary school, time enough to think of that. Suddenly Molemi leaned forward and shouted in anger, not so much at his wife as at the world: "But that is the money for my seed corn! Where do I get it? Where money to mend my plow? And the house, you keep saying there should be a new glass in the window where the piece was broken and the cold wind came in all winter. Glass costs money. Food costs money! You have taken everything for this education, for these children! And more children to get education next year!"

"Perhaps you will have to sell a cow," said Tsholofelo. He began to shout louder that he would not sell a cow, he would never sell a cow! The youngest child, Ketse, stumbled in, a little fat girl wearing blue beads. She was frightened till her mother picked her up and suckled her. Well, thought Tsholofelo, Dineo will just have to wear the Sunday dress for school; she cannot have a gym tunic unless the harvest is good. Perhaps I could put a big patch on that dress. She put back a rand note.

"Thotwe will have to come to the cattle post," said Molemi.

"He is young!" said Tsholofelo, half pleading. He was only seven years old.

"There is nothing else for it," said Molemi, "and he has learned to herd goats. But until he has learned well, I must go back to herding myself. This education! Why does the Chief say we must educate all our children? Look what comes of it. There is no rain!" Then suddenly he said, "If there is no rain they will not go to school!" And he banged with his fist on the top of the biggest of the tin boxes so that it made a loud noise.

Yet that was fair because if the rains did not come there would be no crops and no money. What they had would have to turn into food. But Tsholofelo looked sad and frightened when he banged, and he did not want her to look that way. He took her by the wrists and held her tight and then he hit her a couple of times. That hurt

54

but she did not really mind because he would not have hit her if he had not cared about her so much; she liked to feel that she belonged to him, that they were entirely part of one another, even if it meant the strength and sting of his hand. But she hoped more than ever that there would be rain soon. Oh surely, surely, the rain would come!

·

CHAPTER 4

Shall We Get to School?

BUT THE RAINS CAME in the end, the October rains, with crashes of thunder and lightning, everything swimming and dripping. The river rose with a great brown rush and swept down, wasting its waters. The grass came up and the cattle fed. For a short time everyone was happy; they were hoping that the rains would go on. Molemi hoped, as everyone did, that this might be one of the years when there was good rain, but no, the sky cleared and stayed hard and hot and blue; the clouds that floated high overhead never let drop the rain that they all needed. By the end of December, the early-sown crops were beginning to dry up and wither. Molemi had mended his plow more or less and had plowed. He was late plowing because he had an arrangement with a neighbor about the ox team, and the oxen took a long time to fatten and the ground had almost dried up before Molemi plowed, and his seeds did not come up properly. If everyone could have plowed at once after the rain, with dung plowed into the soil earlier still, it would have been better, but only a few people had tractors, or could afford to hire them. Those who had plowed in winter (that is, in Bechuanaland, between April and August) had a better chance of a crop, but Molemi couldn't see why he should plow twice. If the agricultural demonstrators tried to argue with him, he got angry and shouted at them.

But even with things looking bad, most of the people of Mochudi went out to their lands and tried to make the best of things. People in Bechuanaland grow mabele, which the whites call kaffir-corn, a kind of millet. There are several sorts and the good farmers usually plant two or three kinds, which gives a better chance for something to do well. They grow mealies and beans and sweet cane, and a very few have begun to grow cotton. It is too dry to grow peanuts. Some up-to-date farmers sow their crops in drills, one kind of plant only; but many more still sow in the old way, mixing the seeds. Between the tall plants there are always long trails of watermelon or squash. The women have to hoe constantly once the plants start growing, beginning in the early morning. How handy Dineo was at this already! But no, her mother thought, she shall have education if I have to work twice as hard.

When they went to their lands they drove most of the goats out with them, leaving only a few for Nkoko to look after. Nkoko means Grannie and that is what they all called Molemi's mother. It showed that they respected her. They had a long walk to their lands, the best part of twenty miles, but they were all used to walking; it was not so far as the cattle posts which lay beyond, another ten miles or more. Their mother carried the baby in a goatskin on her back, and Dineo sometimes took the next littlest, who was a boy called Maputso, on her back for half a mile. Maputso means reward in Setswana. Molemi carried his tools and a very old gun, but it was well looked after and still shot properly. Cartridges were expensive; he had only a few and tried not to waste one of them. Tsholofelo carried her hoe and Dineo's small hoe, and any stores they needed in a basket on her head, as well as the baby.

Once they were out on their lands they lived in a round hut, and their other grandmother, Tsholofelo's mother, in another hut. It was a very long carry for water. In Mochudi the borehole was half a mile away, long enough with a full pail on one's head, but at the lands it was farther still and worse water when you got it. Tsholofelo walked easily with a full pail on her head,

there and back, there and back, but Dineo had to steady
it with one hand and Dikeledi, her cousin, could only
manage a pail half full of water, though she tried hard
to work like a big girl. Sometimes Dikeledi missed her
own mother, even though she knew that she was
altogether a daughter for Molemi and Tsholofelo.

Molemi had only a small plot of land; his father had
asked for it from the Chief and had fenced it with
thorns which kept out the cattle. He did not pay rent for
it; it was not his land, nor did he think it ought to be.
The land belonged to the Tribe, and he was one of the
Tribe. But the crops on the land were his. That is, if it
was a reasonably good year when one could get a crop.
After the crops were harvested the thorn fences were
opened, so that cattle could come in and graze on the
stems and old leaves. But there would be little enough
for them this year.

In the hut at the land there were a few blankets and
skin rugs, two or three enamel cups and plates, much
chipped, and a three-legged iron pot over the wood fire.
There was a kettle but it had begun to leak. There were
baskets for putting things into and half-gourds for
drinking from, since there were not enough mugs to go
around. You could hang the mugs on the points of a
dead branch that was stuck in the ground, and the milk
pail was there too, for Molemi had brought in from the
cattle post two cows with calves, which were allowed to

suck after he had milked part away from the cows. One of them was a pretty young cow; he had thought her calf would die, but the rain had come just in time.

The two boys were out at the cattle post and little Thotwe with them. His mother had told them to take great care of him, not to let him walk too many miles and to see that he got plenty of milk. But Thotwe himself was delighted; he grinned from ear to ear; he had taken a step up, he was no longer a child; he would see his uncle Thotwe for whom he was named. He too would tame an ox for himself!

It was nice for the others out at the lands. There were more wild fruits. The marulas were beginning to ripen; you rolled them under your hand on a stone, and then the scented juice spurted out deliciously; then you nibbled around the stone and threw it away. The marula trees with their huge grayed trunks, and leaves like ash leaves, were beautiful, standing green and tall above the flat-topped thorn bushes. But the children thought mostly about the fruit. There were moretlwa berries as well, brownish, growing on a silvery-leafed bush. And there was a wild creeping plant that often grew as a weed among crops, that had a kind of green flat nut that you could roast in the embers of the fire; morama, these were called. Oh, there was plenty to find! But it was scary sometimes in the evening to hear the hyenas, though they were safe enough behind their thorn fence, their own and their neighbors', and so were the cattle behind the heavy dark branch fence of the kraal.

"When I was a boy," said Molemi, "there were lions." He hummed a bit of a song, and then he began to tell about a lion hunt when he was young, and how they had taken the lion skin to the Chief and had got great praise and much beer. But nowadays the lions were all on the western side of the railway line, toward the Kalahari desert where the Bushmen lived. Almost all the lions. You just couldn't quite count on it. And the same for leopards.

At the lands they had old wooden bowls for porridge, which had to be scrubbed out with coarse sandy whitewash; there wasn't water to spare. Dineo made her sister-cousin Dikeledi help her with this. Once she said, in her father's hearing, "When I go to school, she must do it." Was he going to answer? But he said nothing. And he said nothing either when Letsebe killed a snake, hitting it with a stone. Everyone was pleased, because this was a poisonous snake and it might have killed a kid or a hen or even a baby. When it was quite dead, they pulled it about by the tail; all the Bakgatla hate snakes. Letsebe had carried it at arm's length to show his father and said, "When I am at school I shall tell them I killed a snake." And he looked to see how his father would take it. But his father grunted and said nothing that meant either yes or no.

Tsholofelo had been a little anxious about leaving Nkoko, the other grandmother at Mochudi, with nobody to look after her, but Nkoko herself was quite happy. She could not pound for a hungry family but she could pound enough for herself, and they had left her one milk-goat. The neighbors would not leave her lonely. And she had decided that she was going to decorate the walls of the lapa with new patterns in gray and white. She was good at this and she liked doing it when the children were not there to fall over her things.

Perhaps she would make a basket; she knew all the best patterns. They need not be anxious. She was as tough as a wheel ox!

They all went back to Mochudi for Christmas. Most of the family went to the Mission church and sang hymns. At New Year some of the children dressed up and went around the village; Letsebe and some of his friends dressed up as witch doctors. There were a few witch doctors about and old-fashioned people believed in them, but not modern boys like Letsebe, who had been vaccinated for smallpox and who had once been taken to a circus.

There were not many presents, except that some of the shops gave away sweets and biscuits. But there was more visiting than usual, and in the evening when it was cooler, the children's school choirs went around the village singing. One older boy had made a kind of fiddle out of a tea box, with a string on a tall stick that could be pulled tight on to it.

This boy was at the Sunday school, and not only could he play tunes on the fiddle that one could dance the Twist to, but also he knew many English poems by heart and these he would recite while Letsebe and Dineo listened and sometimes giggled, so odd and amusing the sounds were! The meanings of these poems, he said, were difficult and hidden. English was a difficult language. But there was also a language called Latin and another called French. It was possible for people to take them in their final examinations, though he was not doing it. But a scholar like himself had no difficulty with English. He told Letsebe and Pheto some English words like "good-bye" and "blackboard." Some day perhaps they would surprise their teacher by knowing them!

One evening their uncles and aunts were all there and they began to speak of the many branches of the family. At one time, a hundred years ago, they had lived on good land with rivers that flowed all the year round and green pastures, land in what was today called the Transvaal. Some of the cousins still lived there, across in the Republic. There were the Mangopes who lived in the old capital of the Tribe, Moruleng, which the Afrikaners called Saulspoort. But now it was said they had moved, some said to Pretoria or perhaps Rustenberg. The father had been a carpenter, but he had sent his boys to school. The eldest was a teacher; he would be bringing in good money to the family; he would have a nice house and wear a good suit all the time. "But they never come here. It is too hot. They are too comfortable there. They have water coming out of taps. They have lights in the streets."

"But they also have white policemen," said Molemi, "and that is not so good."

"Our family would not get into police trouble."

"Is it possible to know? These police make the trouble where there is none," said Molemi's elder uncle, "but our cousins are quiet people. All the Mangopes were quiet people. Not drinking. Wanting education."

"These police," said big Thotwe, Molemi's lucky brother, "they are blind, they are stupid. They are not altogether awake."

"You cannot count on that," said Molemi. "When you think they are blind then they see most."

"If a man goes into a house where there is someone sleeping," said the elder uncle, quoting a proverb, "it is better to close the door very quietly." And this was something that they all agreed about.

The corn began to sprout but it was thin on the ground; even the weeds did not grow much. If only there could be more rain! They knew and everyone knew that if the rain did not come the corn plants would wither. They would never come into ear. The beans would not come up. There were always some lands where people had left the plowing till too late. They had become discouraged. It would not be worthwhile to plow. Sometimes the clouds would gather, the lightning would play, thick streaks of dreadful light from clouds to ground; there might be a little rain, perhaps only on a few fields. And sometimes it came so hard that it washed the earth away. Everyone longed for soft rain, soft, continuous rain gently feeding the crops. Rain for two days!

By mid-January it was very hot. And Molemi said nothing. "You must not ask me," said Tsholofelo and held Dineo close to her. The two of them, the women of the household, worked among the crops in the early morning. That was the only cool time. All the afternoon you had to sleep. The teachers came back to Mochudi and started getting the schools in order. Suddenly Molemi said to Letsebe and Pheto, "Let's go," and started off toward the school. Her mother gave Dineo a push. "Follow them!" And when Molemi looked around and saw her coming along, he didn't shout at her to go back to the house.

They had a long wait at the school, where the headmaster was enrolling the new boys and girls. There were more girls than boys, because a lot of fathers simply said they needed their sons at the cattle posts. By the time the boys themselves wanted education, it was too late. This was beginning to change but such things take time.

Dozens of children were at the classroom door already; Molemi sat down on his haunches just outside with a bit of cheap tobacco in his pipe. The children whispered to other children and tried to see through into the classrooms. At last it was their turn. With a bad enough grace, Molemi pushed them forward, gave their names and ages to the headmaster and counted out the money, penny by penny. Now all that was left was to get the khaki shorts and shirts for the boys and a big patch of nearly the same color onto Dineo's Sunday dress. Then they would be real schoolchildren!

CHAPTER 5

To Make the Rain Come

THE FIRST FEW DAYS at school they all felt lost. But at last they attached themselves to a teacher and a group. There was no room inside the school; most of the younger classes had to sit on the rocks under the trees. There were lots and lots of other boys and girls, more than one could count. Most of the bigger girls had gym tunics with shirts, or bits of shirts. But many of the younger ones, like Dineo, only had their old dresses. Most of the boys had shorts and shirts or cotton jerseys, mostly handed down from big brothers and a bit torn. None of them had shoes.

There was a blackboard and a teacher wrote things on it, making marks with a chalk; then everyone had to make a noise, all reading together. The children all learned to do this, but it was a long time before they put together the noise and the mark on the blackboard. Nobody thought of asking. Besides, if one asked, then sixty more might have asked, and what would the teacher have done? The entrance classes were up to 90 children. Sometimes they could see birds in the trees, and beyond was the village and the sounds of life going on, people shouting, goats or sheep bleating, oxen moving and the creaking of carts, while they had to sit still. After a while you got hungry. Most children came to school without eating, half of them starting off before seven in the morning. The hungriest dropped asleep; it was the best way out of it. The older children came in the morning, the younger in the afternoon; in this way, twice as many children could be taught.

All these schools had been built by the Tribe, though now the Government helped with repairs and teachers' salaries. Those who had built them thought that once you had the school, the worst was over. Everyone had helped to build. When the Regent Isang built the school that is called after him, he said: "I want work, not money." He wanted money too and got it; the men went to work as far south as the Cape to earn money for building the school. But above all he wanted work. The men made the bricks and the lime plaster. He called chiefly on his own royal family and on his own initiation group. For among the Bakgatla and many other peoples, when you become a man, truly one of the Tribe, you go through a period of initiation, of living out in the open, running down game, little sleep, learning songs which are so packed with meaning that they are far more than ordinary songs; above all one special song which is your own. An older initiation group—they are called regiments when people speak in English, and of course there was a time when they *were* regiments, ready for war—looks after them. This older group teaches them songs and beats them when they forget; it makes them run. There are tests of courage and endurance. In the end the group comes back

feeling that now they are truly men. Molemi had been in such a group and it still meant much to him; people in the same group would help one another. Tsholofelo, too, had been in a women's regiment, and they remained friendly and sometimes sang their songs together, especially when they were doing the same work or joining in some women's occasion, all hoeing or all making the floor of a lapa.

But all this was many years ahead for the children, something to do with being grown up. Meanwhile they were at school. After a few weeks they began to put together questions and answers; if the teacher asked a certain thing, you answered in a certain way. Sometimes, even, you could put your hand up. That was nice. That was being at school. And when you put your hand up, you must not giggle; you must answer properly.

But meanwhile Molemi and Tsholofelo and the rest of the family went back to the lands. The sun was hot, burning up the crops; there was so little rain. If there was a storm it would break somewhere and water a few lands, but there was never rain all over everywhere. The clouds might gather, the lightning play around the horizon, you could even smell the rain a mile away, but it might miss you and your thirsty crops altogether. But Tsholofelo felt she had to be there; it was her work to hoe, with the other grandmother. What if there were no weeds because there had been no rain? Her place was on the land. Everyone went to the lands during the crop time. They always had.

But what about the children? Well, the grandmother would have to look after them. She and Dineo could pound enough mabele corn for porridge. The old woman could see that it did not burn in the pot. The boys would catch and milk the milk goat. And the three children would all walk out to the lands on Friday evening and walk back on Sunday evening, carrying back whatever their mother had made for them. They had taken off their good school clothes and walked almost naked. It was nearly twenty miles and it was very, very seldom that they met a truck going the same way which could give them a lift. There are not many trucks in Mochudi and usually several of them have broken down. Besides, the last part of the walk was along a winding dust path, cruelly hot on the feet and full of thorns. But their feet were hard.

When they got to the kraal and heard the lowing of the cattle, they knew they were almost there. Around one more corner was the thorn fence and inside they could lie on the ground and rest. Perhaps there would be delicious lumpy sour milk; there might be some kind of vegetables, perhaps boiled squash; there might even be meat. There would surely be a stick of sweet cane to chew and spit out, juicy and lovely; there would be boiled mealies. And there would be the rest of the family. Dineo cuddled the little ones, especially Mosidi. That is a name that means the pounder of corn. And when Mosidi whisked the floor of the hut clean, going properly into the corners and chasing out the ants and beetles, Dineo praised her and sang her little songs.

Often the grandmother told them stories. She told them about the woodpecker, and she told them about the dog who was given a letter to call the other dogs to a meeting. The dogs were going to get together and claim their freedom from men. They were going to eat all the meat, not just help the men to hunt and then get the worst bits! But what happened? The messenger dog tucked the letter under his tail and he ran and ran. But then he came to a river and while he was swimming across, the water took the letter away. The letter was gone, altogether gone. But the rest of the dogs knew that there should be a letter coming to them, and that is why when two dogs meet, you will always see them smelling one another's tails, in case the letter is still there.

Meanwhile, little Thotwe was out at the cattle post. He was the youngest of the boys and they played all sorts of tricks on him, until gradually he learned how to get out of being teased and how to play tricks back. And his uncles saw that he got his share of meat and milk. But he was still afraid to take the cattle too far in case he got lost. Once he had been lost and had been very frightened. He had run and called and had begun to think of leopards and hyenas. It turned out that he was really quite close to the kraal and everyone had laughed at him.

All the children scared the birds off the scarce corn. Even Moputso ran and shouted and clapped his hands till he got tired and fell on the ground and slept.

Dikeledi helped with the pounding, but she wasn't very big. Her thin little arms only just lifted the pestle. She wasn't as useful as Dineo; but then, Tsholofelo kept saying to herself, Dineo is at school, I have a daughter who is a schoolgirl. She asked them about school, were they obedient to the teacher? Yes, they said. They smoothed out a piece of sand, and wrote with their fingers: A.B.C.D. One day they would be able to write all the letters. Numbers were more difficult; they curled up and went the wrong way round. But they could manage I. "I like school very much," said Letsebe. But Pheto wasn't saying. Dineo looked at her mother and didn't even need to say how much she liked it. Except for not having a gym tunic.

On Friday night they always slept long, curled up on their goatskin rugs on the floor of the hut. If Tsholofelo lifted an arm of one of them it hung loose and dropped. "If things go badly, perhaps the school will give them porridge," Tsholofelo said. "Unless the rains come in time," said Molemi. For people thought about the rain almost all the time. It meant life or death. It did not mean it quite so certainly nowadays, because Oxfam sent in bags of meal which had been fortified with proteins so that it fed the schoolchildren at least. But you cannot learn very well on a cup of meal a day.

But what could you do about the rain except hope? Some people said there were things that could be done. But was that true? You looked at the sky and you talked about years when there had been good rain: not many years, but they were remembered. Ten years ago. Fifteen years. You thought that perhaps tomorrow—or the next day—but always the cruel sun struck down, taking your strength as it took the strength of the plants and the cattle.

The children took back what there was for them on Sunday evening, a few mealies, one or two squashes. Later on there would be watermelons, but they were still hard and hollow when you tapped them. Still the children went and looked at them, counting how many there would be. But a good watermelon needs rain to swell it.

It would be dark before they were back at Mochudi, the orange gold fading out of the sky, the come-to-supper star showing first of all the many stars that powdered the night. But would there be supper, or would their grandmother be asleep? "Nkoko, Nkoko!"

they would call. That was Grannie, their own Grannie. She might have porridge for them; someone would perhaps have milked the goat and there would be milk. Yet they were too hot and tired to eat much; mostly they wanted to drink, and sometimes there was no water. Their grandmother was too old for the long carry to the borehole. Sometimes a neighbor remembered to bring her a pail of water, sometimes she didn't. If there was no water, Dineo would set off for the borehole, tired as she was.

But at least their Nkoko at home at Mochudi, like their other grandmother on the lands, told them stories. She told them about the cow that was to be driven over the river, but wouldn't budge. The stick wouldn't beat the cow, the ants wouldn't eat the stick, the fire wouldn't burn the ants, the water wouldn't quench the fire and so on. Or she would tell them about the clever hare, the noble lion that was king of the beasts but could be taken in by the fox, the wicked hyena, and the dreadful beast that went oompa-oompa, that was just a lump of flesh, destroying everything. And the children breathed quickly and huddled together, wondering if they could hear the beast coming; but at the same time they were sure that the clever hare, although it was so small, would be able to get the better of the great dreadful beast.

Sometimes the grandmother told them stories out of

their own past, and this was interesting because she remembered exactly what had been said, yes, even about people who had been dead before she was born. All was remembered, the brave and clever answer, the judgment in Kgotla in which this or that man or woman had got their rights. There had been a case where she herself had been a witness, and she often talked about this. It was about an inheritance and had the mother been properly married? "Yes," said Nkoko, "certainly she had been, and it was I who proved it. I remember the bogadi cattle." She told them about one which was most beautifully spotted, the pride of the kraal. And Nkoko spoke lovingly about this cow, which had so long been dead.

But on Sunday evenings the children were tired. Dineo began to slide down onto the floor. She would have liked to wash her dusty feet, but there was no water for that. But at least Nkoko had usually washed their school clothes on Friday evening, at any rate Dineo's dress, so that all should be ready at dawn on Monday, when they woke to cocks crowing, dogs barking, birdsong and people laughing and shouting. But there was no hurry for them. They could watch the ox teams go past with a jingle and clatter and the crack of the long whip. They could watch the bigger girls and boys go by to school with their books in their hands or on their heads. So many books and perhaps even an inkpot, for these students had learned to write with ink. It looks smart to balance an inkpot on one's head. Then everyone knows that one is a schoolgirl.

But Dineo had to go to the borehole and wait, sometimes for an hour, until she could fill the pail and bring it back much heavier than an inkpot. While she waited she listened to the other women and girls talking. She heard who was expecting a baby and who was likely to be married. She heard about illness and death and sometimes about bewitchment; she got to know the price of meat and meal. In a bad year people have to buy more from the shops. And always, always, there was talk about the rain and how could it be made to come.

It seemed to her that some of the women were talking about the church and how it would be best if all came together for a day of prayer. The headman should go and make the Chief have this done. But others said no, there were ways which used to work well. Did they not remember that year, just after the men came back from the war against the Germans, the war for which the English had thanked them, and there was no rain? That year the women had taken things into their own hands and there had been good rain. One of them hummed a line from a song and others nodded.

And while Dineo was getting water, and afterwards pounding meal, Letsebe and Pheto were away gathering wood. They had to go far, for all the wood close to the house had been taken; their Nkoko scolded them if they let her run out of wood. They carried back big branches, proudly, and sometimes they repeated things they had learned by heart at school, laughing over them. There were word songs and arithmetic songs. Oh, lots of singing at school!

In the hottest weeks nobody could play; it was bad enough doing physical exercises before school, but at least that was before the hard strike of the sun. After school they could hardly drag themselves along to do the necessary things. But when it was full moon they played games in the moonlight, hide-and-seek and singing games. They all sang easily, picking up the tunes of English songs even though the words meant nothing. The moonlight was so bright that you could see colors; you could be sure you wouldn't tread on a snake. Sometimes, too, they sat around and told one another stories, often quite frightening stories with witches in them. Many of these stories had little songs running through them. But they did this even more in winter when they sat around the fires.

One day Letsebe's grandmother said to him, "Get me some clay from the river."

"Which clay, Nkoko?" asked Letsebe.

She told him carefully. He brought along a great lump; she had some pieces of the right rock pounded.

Then one evening she began to teach Dineo how to make a pot. You could do it two ways. Either you could coil ribbons of clay and then smooth them over, or you could build up the pot with your fingers inside. But either way you must keep the pot smooth and even, with a nice rim and the neck coming in from it. "That is how we make pots. Other people make other pots, but the pot that a Mokgatla woman makes is the most beautiful."

Some of her pots had patterns scratched on them, but the pattern mattered less than the shape. Dineo made one which more or less satisfied her grandmother. It was put to dry. The big red beer pots were always fired but that was a big business, with much talk and preparation. The boys looked on at the women's pots. Then they took bits of clay and began to make cows. These had very short legs but very long horns; some of them were more horns than cow. They too were put to dry; then they could fight one another, or other boys' cows!

Clouds gathered in the evening but never broke. "Something will have to be done," said their grandmother. "Soon it will be too late to plow."

It is just possible to get a crop if you plow during the first ten days of February and many people had left it. There was much complaining, too, about the prices you got four oxen from the Government. Perhaps they were better than the prices you used to get from the traders but still you couldn't go and bargain. These were long-legged, strong Afrikander or Tswana cattle, though a few go-ahead farmers had crossed them with Brahmans or Red Devon or Herefords. But these had to be better looked after, sprayed and inoculated against disease. The team oxen that were worked every day were named and petted, but most of them ran almost wild, except that the herd boys had a few tamed for their own riding. That was something Letsebe missed now he was at school.

Their Aunt Modie had a Sunday school class, and they went to this too; it was usually held under a tree, and again there were things one said in chorus. Sometimes they went to it, sometimes not. They were supposed to pay pennies for little books, but they did not have pennies. Their aunt gave them books all the same. Once one of their uncles gave them each a penny, but they did not think about books; they ran to the shop and bought pink and yellow sweets, the kind you get most of. It was nice to be in the shop with money and to see all the things that could be bought, dresses and shoes and shirts and lamps, knives and canned meat and piles of enamel bowls. Even clocks! And proper gym tunics, such as schoolgirls should wear. There were thin places in Dineo's dress that tore in a moment if someone pulled at her in the playground. It had been worn so long and washed so often.

There came a day when there was much bustle.
Several of the women who were in the same mophato
—the same regiment—as Nkoko came over to see her.
Dineo hung about on the edge of the group, but they
chased her away. Some of them brought bundles of

leaves. At first Nkoko shook her head but in a while she agreed that these were the right leaves.

The next day the women got together and began singing up at the Chief's house; they were in their best clothes and Gasetswane herself, the Chief's mother, was leading them, wearing leaves tied around her head; these were the same that Nkoko and her friends, the elder women of the Tribe, had decided were the right leaves. Dineo joined them and so did a lot of little girls; they waited quite quietly around the edge, some of them sucking marulas, while the women started singing. Dineo came close to her cousin Nkomeng and whispered, "What happens?"

Nkomeng said, "They will pray for rain."

Dineo said, puzzled, "But do they not pray in the church?"

"This is a different kind of prayer," Nkomeng said.

"A prayer to Modimo, to God?" asked Dineo anxiously.

"Yes, yes," said Nkomeng, "but this is the old way before there were churches."

"Is there a new way?" Dineo asked.

"The new way," said Nkomeng, "is with airplanes that fly in the sky and drop something on the clouds. It does not have anything to do with Modimo. At school I saw a picture of this." Nkomeng is a very odd name; it means, Threaten but don't strike.

But Dineo thought this sounded altogether too strange. The bustle subsided; the women formed up into a big group and began to sing as they moved downhill—women wearing green leaves on their heads. Certainly it was a kind of prayer that they were singing. They asked for rain. Pula, pula: rain, rain. The girls and children followed them. They went from one ward of Mochudi to the next. At each ward they sang their song in the kgotla, the meeting place. Other women came running out of the houses to join them. But after a while Nkomeng shrugged her shoulders and turned away and left them.

When they came down into the center of Mochudi, they went to the great kraal where Chief Molefi lies buried somewhere under the churning hoofs of cattle, forever close to kgotla, to his people. Here they took off their crowns of green leaves and heaped them up. Someone gave Gasetswane a half-gourd of water and she sprinkled the leaves while all sang loudly and many looked at the sky. Then there was a scuffle and a shouting and laughing, and all of them at once rushed out and surrounded Chief Linchwe, where he sat in kgotla, listening to a case and not paying attention to the women because he did not believe that what they were doing would bring rain. They began to beat him, not hard, but there were many of them and he broke through them and ran into the office, and when they all shouted under his window, that was the window he shut.

It did not rain at once but it rained in a day or two. That meant that those who believe in this kind of prayer felt that they had brought the rain, but those who did not believe it said that the prayer had nothing to do with the rain. But even so, it was not enough rain. It only lasted for half an hour and the ground soon dried up again. Nkoko said that there must have been certain things not done right, and especially that the Chief should have been more beaten by the women. "I could have beaten him well!" said Nkoko, and laughed.

But the heat went on, bearing down on everything. They could hardly keep awake at school. They drank water and then the boys went to sleep in the shade of the house. Dineo had got hold of a piece of string which the shop had thrown out and was playing *malepa,* the string game. She made a figure exactly the same as cat's cradle, then she made Naledi, the star. Then she made the saw figure, holding the long end on her toe and sawing gently; it seemed to take her mind off the heat. Then two of her uncles came in, to talk to their mother. Uncles are important in Mochudi; you have to consult them and pay attention to them. Thotwe was the lucky uncle who helped with one of the trucks and sometimes had spare pennies; the other was Mooki, the unlucky uncle who never seemed to do much and always smelled a little of beer whatever time of day it was.

"The Ward has told the Chief that they will secede," said Thotwe, the lucky uncle.

Nkoko nodded. "So now he will see about the rain. That is good. That is better than the women."

"He has named a day for public prayer."

"In the church?" said the old lady doubtfully, scratching herself and frowning.

"No, in kgotla. All the schools must come too."

"That is not enough," she said, "he should kill an ox."

"We are Christians now. God should listen to us. We do not need to kill oxen," said Thotwe. "You should not have such thoughts, Nkoko."

"We can take no chances when it comes to the rain," she said. "But I suppose the Chief is like the rest of you, turned away from his ancestors and all that should be done. No wonder it is so hot."

"We shall take you," said Thotwe, "then you will see the praying."

"How?" she said.

"I will get the truck to come," said Thotwe, "then we will hoist you on. We will all come. If we can get a cow on that truck, we can get you, Nkoko."

It seemed likely to Dineo that if her grandmother went on the truck she would go too. Perhaps not the boys! Thotwe dug in his pocket and found her a sweet. That too helped her not to think of how hot it was.

The day of the prayer came around. When the Ward

told the Chief they were going to secede, it meant that he had to do something about the rain. He was the mediator between his Tribe and whatever powers there were. In the old days he might have done various things, including the sacrifice of an ox. And indeed there had been a time when the sacrifice was a very black boy. Today his duty was to call together the Tribe for mass prayer.

There is a kind of rough square between the terrace with the tribal office, through the windows of which one can see such things as typewriters and telephones, and the deep and solid wooden shelter where the elders of the Tribe meet their Chief to discuss cases and see that justice is done and the moral order is restored. At one side are notice boards saying on what day of the week one may find the van from the bank there. On the other side is the stone wall of the great kraal where the Chief's father was buried. Two kinds of lives and two kinds of social order meet there.

But on the day of the prayer it was crowded, packed with people, a few sitting on benches, or on folding chairs that they had brought with them, but most on the ground. The grandmother had been hoisted onto the truck, with Dineo to hold on to her, for it was rough going. Even the main road has deep pits and ruts in it and the truck rocked and pitched. She had put on a great blue apron, frilled and tucked, much washed; she had a clean head-scarf. But Dineo had only the same dress. The whole middle of the square was filled with children sitting on the ground, packed close. Dineo dived in among the girls. Letsebe and Pheto were at the other side among the little boys. Opposite them under the kgotla shelter, behind a table, was the Chief; beside him were the important people, his uncles and senior people in the Tribe and the Church. The Chief looked at them and you could not tell at all what he was thinking, or whether he believed in this any more than be believed in what the women had done. All the staff of the Tribal Office was there. If the telephone were to ring, it would not be answered. The teachers were there. All the stores were shut and the storekeepers had come down to pray.

The women all wore colored head-scarfs, and often aprons over their dresses; many carried babies, but the babies were good and hardly cried. People were jumbled together: the royal family and the rest of the Tribe: the people with cars of their own and the ragged ones who had not even a pair of sandals. Many had come from the lands. Molemi himself arrived, just in time. Then there was hymn singing and prayer and Bible reading, all in Tswana so that it was entirely understood. The hymns were beautifully harmonized and floated up, wistfully hoping for the gift of rain. Here were the innocent people, the hungry children:

could God withhold the rain they needed for life? All bowed their heads in prayer and the children groveled on the ground, their heads in the dust. Would this not reach wherever the rains were kept and loosed?

But the sun blazed down on them. Suddenly the meeting for prayer was over. People looked hopefully at the sky. Nkoko was hoisted back on the truck. The children were chased back to school. The uncles were over again that evening to talk to the old lady. "Will it rain now?" Letsebe asked. "It will certainly rain," said his uncle. But Nkoko still thought that the Chief should have done other things. The Church was powerful, yes, but it did not control everything.

When the children came back from school the next day, they found their father and the uncles talking; there was also a senior uncle, Nkoko's brother, who did not often leave his house. Even their Sunday school aunt Modie was there, dabbing at her eyes. They had a copy of the *Rand Daily Mail* and they were talking about something in it, jabbing at it with their fingers. "It cannot be our cousins," said Uncle Thotwe, "they would not do such things." He looked around, but nobody agreed with him. A friend of the family who worked for the contractors in Gaberones, the big town, the new capital of Bechuanaland where they got newspapers every day, had seen this thing and asked one of the trucks to take the paper to Mochudi and give it quickly to those whom it concerned.

"It is the same name. The son was a teacher," said Molemi gloomily. The others nodded. And then he read through the paragraph again, slowly, whispering the words to himself: "Suppression of Communism—what is that?"

"It is their name in the Republic for whatever they do not like," the senior uncle said and they all listened to him. "Whatever they say is against the Afrikaners, that

is called Communism. But perhaps it is not our cousins' family."

"It is the same name," said Thotwe, for now he too agreed. "Joseph Mangope. And to give a teacher ten years' imprisonment! And all for meeting a few friends and singing a song! Which of us has not done that?"

"Here in Bechuanaland we could sing 'God Save Africa' and it would not be Communism. There it is different. And to have beaten him before imprisonment, eight strokes, to do that to a teacher is—is—" Molemi could not think of the words which would show how he felt, what shame and pain.

Aunt Modie said, "To beat a teacher is against God." And this was something that all of them agreed to.

"They are mad," said Thotwe.

"They are certainly mad," said Molemi, "but I am much afraid that it is our cousins."

CHAPTER 6

Flight Toward Freedom

PETRUS HAD SO MUCH wanted to go with his brother to the house at the far side of the location, and at last Joseph looked at him as though he was measuring to see if Petrus was a man, and said, yes, he could come. Joseph was beginning to feel safe again; he had been so careful. He had kept his mouth shut at school, or thought he had. He had taught no geography that was not in the Bantu Education syllabus. Sampson did not seem to be watching him. Perhaps he was wrong about Sampson. Why should anyone want to inform? Besides, he had done nothing illegal. Well, scarcely illegal, but you never knew where the mesh was being tightened, what new laws they were passing. But none of them had plotted revolution. They did not plan to kill anyone. What good would it have done if they had been able to? All they wanted was so little, a small bit of pride and hope, a tiny light at the far end of the future.

So Petrus went with his brother, neither of them speaking in the road, except about ordinary things, a new jazz record that they had both heard, half a cent off the pink fizzy drink. And now he was sitting, not with the men at the table, but on a little stool by the kitchen door. There was a letter which was being passed around, a letter from outside, about a speech that had been made, an article that would be written and published; at the end Joseph took it and put it inside his coat. It said so little yet it was like something magic and warming. Then they spoke of a man who seemed interested, could they trust him? No, they said, not now, not yet. It was terrible not to be able to trust one's own people. But there it was. And Petrus listened and seemed to be understanding more and more.

Then they spoke of certain ones who were in prison, of help they could perhaps give to their children. One of the others said, "There is money from overseas, money sent by white people to help."

"Do you think that can be true?" said Joseph's friend, the clerk in the town hall. "Would they do that—whites?"

One of the others said, angrily, "They are rich."

"When were their riches for us?" said the clerk.

But Joseph said, "I am sure. They are different, these ones, although they are white. They are truly our friends. They do not even want to do to us the things the Afrikaners do to us here."

"We cannot even say it is all the Afrikaners," said another, an elderly man who sometimes preached in their church. "A woman spoke to me the other day, perhaps she was a Black Sash."

"One woman!" said the clerk. "Does that make up?" He looked at the table, and then he began to speak of how his baas had come on him earlier that day, calling him dishonest, dirty, a lying kaffir—"And for a mistake in the books that one of *them* made!" Hurt, hurt, hurt. Others spoke the same way, at last able to speak of swallowed insults, of a tone in the voice that they could not explain; they spoke low about being helpless, about everything getting worse and more and more laws being made by the Afrikaners, the whites, who were both so afraid and so cruel. You could not be so cruel, surely, unless you were also afraid?

And then, to comfort themselves, they began to sing, swaying their heads, and Petrus joined in. They sang first very softly, but then not so softly, one or two of the songs. And it was then that the thin wood of the door splintered and the police were in.

Somebody put an arm through from the kitchen and yanked Petrus right off his stool and hustled him through the back door and into a little patch of mealies where they crouched right down behind the leaves. It was only then that Petrus began to know what had happened. He wanted to run back, to kill—but they held him. "No good," they said. "Keep quiet, keep down or you will kill us all!"

Behind Petrus a man whispered, "That snake Sampson! To do this to his teacher!" And Petrus felt a weight in his stomach, a sickness. So it was Sampson after all. He could not know what was happening in the house, only heard two screams, men's screams so much worse than women's, but did not know if one was his brother. Then the police van driving off. One of the men who was holding him said, "Run home, quick! The back way, over the fence. Say you have been there all the time. They may come. But they will not be certain. One kaffir is like another! Make a story if they come, Petrus! No need for two of the family to be taken, go home!"

Two of them dragged him by the wrists, sobbing, and pushed him over the fence. One of them got him to the house, shoved him through the door and told his mother; she twisted her apron in her hands, listening. "So it has come," she said, "I knew—" And then, "No, he must go, they will look for him, I know them. Try to keep them off—ten minutes—" and then she was going to all the places in the house where he knew she kept money: the can at the back of the drawer; under her pillow; inside the clock that didn't go. She made the money quickly into a little bundle and folded it into a piece of cloth, then stitched it into the top of his shorts. He could hardly hear her speak because his breath was coming so short and troubled. She was telling him things; she shook him to make him listen. "Petrus, you must go. They will get you if you stay. Even a child is not safe from them! Even a child." And then, "Remember the name. Remember you are a Mokgatla. Remember Mochudi. You have cousins there. They will take you in. Your uncle is called Molemi. But the money, the money is for school. You must go on, must be like your brother Joseph. Remember him. Remember him always. I will try to send more. You must write to me. You must get an education. It is what your brother Joseph wanted. Try not to spend one penny till you get to education! Somehow, I will send more." She was making up food now, opening a can of corned beef, making a big sandwich.

He suddenly came awake: "Mother, how will you live?"

She said, "I will live, Petrus my son. The Lord will perhaps provide. There are things I can sell. I can help in a shop, do washing. Oh, much I can do! There is still the little Rebecca and the little Luke. Now listen, my son, you cannot cross at the gates. You have no papers. It is two days' walking. More. Even when you are across, it is not safe. Not until you find your cousins. Remember Mochudi. Remember Molemi."

95

"Molemi, Mochudi," muttered Petrus, but all the time he could only think of what must be happening to his brother. He knew. They all knew. They saw it in the back of their minds. A police boot going in to kick.

His mother was tying it all together, the half loaf with the corned beef in it, an apple, a small packet of sugar and tea. "You might come to someone's fire at night," she said. A clean shirt. A small piece of soap. All tied into an old *doek,* a head-scarf.

"My schoolbooks?" he said.

She shook her head. "Too heavy. They will do for your sister in two years' time. You, Petrus, you must keep all you have learned in your head. Say things over as you walk. Say your tables. They will shorten the way."

Suddenly there was the sound of an engine and wheels outside. Petrus grabbed the bundle and was off through the other door, ready to jump the fence. But his mother called him back, "Quick, son, into the back of the truck. Under the sacks. Our friends will take you five miles down the road. Quick! I have to find those English books now, bury them in the garden!"

"Oh Mother, Mother—"

"Greet the cousins for me. So. The sacks. Can you breathe? Go well, my son, go well!"

The truck was going fast, bumping over ruts and potholes, out of the town. Three or four men in at the back, talking, singing. Did they know he was there?

Most likely. The truck stopped: white voices, argument. A white man stumping about in the back. The weight of a boot on his leg, but he did not let it move and the stupid boot never felt it was standing on flesh. The man with the boot jumping down heavily, curses, the truck going on.

Petrus worked himself a little hole between the sacks so that he could breathe. Then for a few minutes he fell asleep. It had all been too much. One minute, thinking and feeling about Africa, their mother, their great mother whom they loved so much. And the next, the

door smashed open, the police bursting in like terrible elephants, like a nightmare. Joseph getting to his feet and a policeman taking a swing at him. And then, nothing, nothing. He did not know.

And now, what? Would his mother bury the English books from the chest of drawers in time? He should have stayed and helped her. No, she wanted him to go. And what was ahead? Next week, the other teacher at the school had said, they would start fractions. But next week would never come now. It would be an altogether different next week. If it came. If he got there. Got to Mochudi.

The truck stopped, crunched to a standstill. It had to turn off now to a farm, where it was delivering the sacks and some other things, a metal window frame, some spare parts. It would pick up pumpkins, peaches, some green mealies. And there was the road ahead and Petrus must walk.

There was a kind of path at the side of the road and Petrus thought he had better save his shoes; he took them off, knotted the laces and hung them around his neck. He was beginning to know that it might be a very long time before he got new shoes. There were flowers beside the path; he picked one or two, then dropped them. The road was still hilly but soon it would wind down into the flatland. Ahead of him the sun was still hot and steady, but soon it would be dropping. And then?

A few trucks passed, once a heavy car with a white man driving it and his whole family with him. But he was watching for a police car. When it came he was quite simply walking the other way, a careless, barefoot boy, his bundle in the ditch. It passed and he turned, and he would not think what it would have been like if they had caught him. Fortunately most whites are not very good at telling one African from another, one little kaffir brat, one black monkey. He went on, saying the seven times table to himself. And now the western sun was low and a golden color coming into the sky. Soon it would be dark.

He looked about him nervously. He was a town boy. He didn't know what there might be at night. Hyenas, jackals. Not lions, no, no, but—well, he didn't know. He looked for a small house, a house with a light and smoke coming out of it, a house with a yard where he could sleep at least under the shelter of a wall.

He turned off the road, thinking of a story to tell. Well, why not, he was going to live with his cousins in Bechuanaland. No need to tell a lie when the truth was cheap. He chose a small, poor-looking house and spoke to the woman from a little distance, asking if he might sleep by her fire. "Yes, you can sleep," she said, "but you must carry my water."

Queer to be doing something so peacable as carrying water! It didn't seem to be true. If it was true, the other thing couldn't be true. He began to make a game that his brother was waiting for him, would jump out the next time he carried the pail back. But nothing happened. And then, when it was quite dark and nobody could see, he began to cry softly to himself, and he went to sleep alone by the smoldering dead end of the fire.

In the morning the woman gave him a cup of tea; this way he saved his own. He had wondered if she would say anything about the arrest—the arrest of a teacher. But nobody in that little group of houses had a radio. If things happened elsewhere, they did not really happen.

He walked on. Now he was down on the plain; it was hotter. Far ahead was Bechuanaland. He tried to remember all he had heard about it, how it was a dry, hard, poor country. Once he had heard the storekeeper for whom he sometimes ran errands saying that the people were ragged, fierce-looking, so hungry they'd eat a pair of shoes. And his cousins—would they know anything at all about him? How was he to find them? It all seemed impossible.

At first there were barbed-wire fences along the road at both sides. Behind the fences there were sometimes crops—mealies, beans, mabele, tobacco even—white farmers' crops that must not be touched. But sometimes there was nothing but bush, not cut or improved. Petrus remembered something his brother had told him, out of this history that was not like school history. Once the land of Africa had not been fenced; it had not been claimed by anyone. Men and boys drove their cattle freely over it. Then the voortrekkers had come and said that it belonged to them. And later others of the Dutch. So that now there was hardly any free land left. Not, at least, good grazing land. Only land that was too poor and dry and stony for the Dutch farmers to want it. Petrus had only lately begun to understand that, because the schoolbooks talked all the time about the heroism of the voortrekkers, reclaiming land from the wilderness and the savages. There was that picture of the laager and the men in big hats firing rifles with puffs of smoke. When his brother said that these men were firing at his own ancestors, he did not entirely believe it. But now he began to think that it might be true and he hated the barbed-wire fences between him and the bush.

But there were gaps here and there. Luckily it was at a gap that he heard a car coming and ducked in behind thorn bushes and lay there. It was the police car again. So, he thought, I must get off the road.

The sun was almost overhead, no help in getting a direction. It didn't matter which side of the road he took; he would not be able to tell until late whether he was heading west. If only he could get a drink before starting off! The sun had dried him up. He thought of the cup of tea he had drunk hours ago. If only he could find a house or a hut well off the road. He ate the apple, which helped for a little while.

In a bit he put on his shoes. His feet were not tough

enough yet for bush walking on thick hot dust and thorns and spikes. Suddenly he came to a barbed-wire fence across the way he was going. For a time he followed it, then changed his mind and rolled under it. He kept a lookout for anything that might be food or drink. Above all drink. But there seemed to be nothing. Only once a tree with some large greenish fruits. But how was he to know? They might be poison. Then a good way off he saw a great green tree and thought that at least he would lie down under it and sleep. When he woke up he would be able to tell if he was going west.

It seemed to take a long time to get to the tree, pushing past thorn bushes or dodging around them. There were big grasshoppers and lizards bobbing on the rocks, and once he saw a snake ahead of him, wriggling away, pushing the dust aside as it went. But at last he was there, and strewn all over the ground under the tree were hundreds of yellow-green fruits. He wasn't sure, he had never seen a wild marula tree. But these must be the same; he picked one up and bit it, yes it was the same! Then he sat down among them and picked up and bit into a dozen or more. From under the horny skin the juice shot into his thirsty mouth. He sucked the pits; sucking, he fell asleep.

When he woke he was still thirsty and a little headachy from eating all those marulas; now at sundown he could tell the west and knew he had been walking too far south, turned by the fence. He had better walk into the setting sun. He put some more marulas into the front of his shirt. But where would he sleep? He had seen no people since he started walking. He began to listen. If he could hear a cowbell, even, or a goat bleating! Anything familiar. But the grasshoppers were beginning to make a noise so loud, so startling, it was like something on purpose. Then as it began to get dark, he found another fence. So was he inside or outside someone's piece of land?

Thinking of this, his legs and feet began to ache so that he could hardly take another step. He moved back from the fence, behind some low bushes, took off his shoes. There was a thin place coming in one of them. He had better walk barefoot and get used to it. And he thought suddenly of his brother telling the boy David how in the old days the hero Chaka made his *impis* drill and dance on thorns so that their feet should become forever unafraid. Who would coach David now? No one. No one. The boys would forget how to play soccer properly. Would they know that this had been brought on them by one of themselves, by Sampson? And if they knew, would they do anything? No, they would be afraid. Always, always afraid.

He scooped out a hole for his hip and put his head down on his bundle. The dust was warm. The stars arched far overhead as though he could drop upward into pools of light. Blinking at them, he fell asleep.

He woke to confusion, pale dawn, bleating, all

around him goats, white, brown, yellow, spotted, then standing back from then a boy about his own age, wearing tattered shorts and carrying a stick. Petrus greeted him and felt his mouth dry. Could he have a small drink from one of the goats? The other boy looked around, then nodded and brought over by one horn a big old she-goat as tame as a table. Petrus knelt quickly and squirted the milk into his own mouth, gulping it down. Then the boy held up his hand. "Enough. Or the baas will notice."

"White baas? Where is he?"

The boy pointed. And there, down in a green hollow of beans and mealies, was a biggish tin-roofed house with sunflowers around it. "Do you look for work?" the boy asked.

But Petrus shook his head, only hoping that no news of his brother or himself had got to this house. It must be a long way from the main road, but there was a brown rutted track going to the front of it. "I go to visit my cousins," he said, "at Mochudi."

"Ah, that," said the boy, "on the other side. And not by the road. But you have taken the wrong way. Look." He began to scratch in the dust. "Here is the Kgatleng. Here Mochudi. Here the big road. If you had gone off to that side you would have crossed the river and all would have been easy. Now, I think you will have a long walk."

"How long?"

"A day. Perhaps more. You have the hills to get past. But once you are across, you are across. Can ask your way."

"And the hills?"

"Do not get eaten by a leopard." The boy grinned. "There is a track from here toward the border. I will show you. I too have cousins on the far side. Once we crossed by the road, easily, and now there is this stupidity. I am a Mokgatla."

"I too," said Petrus, and suddenly knew that this mattered, in a way he had never known back home. The warm goat's milk swirled in his stomach. As they went quickly along the fence, he felt a little sick but also a little happy. "Wait," he said and undid the bundle, then broke two pieces off the bread with the corned beef in it and gave one to the boy. That left only one lump, the size of half a fist. The bread was dry and crumbly, but it was food: food for a friend.

CHAPTER 7

A Chief on a Horse

THE TRACK WAS NOT very easy to follow; it cornered its way around fences and land with crops. Whenever he saw a house of the whites, Petrus kept very clear; once or twice he saw a white man, but he dodged away among the bushes. Several times he lost the track and had to get back to it. And again he got terribly thirsty as the sun struck down, but this time he saw no marula tree. Yet he thought he must be close to the border— there were hills ahead, the kind of country that white farmers do not want so much. That must be Bechuanaland.

Then suddenly he saw the boundary fence, ten feet of barbed wire closely set. He stood and stared at it. What to do now?

He walked a little way along it, wondering how to climb. At the far side it seemed to be the same: dry bush, rocks, a few trees. And yet it would be different. Then he heard trotting hoofs and hurried back until he was well out of sight. The police hoofs clattered on, with a word or two in loud Afrikaans, the assured, owning police voices. He put his face down into his hands and shook with fear and anger and the thought of his brother whom they had taken. What was happening to him, what?

There was a woman coming along the path, carrying a big piece of firewood. He did not dodge her; she must be of his people. He stood and greeted her. She looked at him quietly, then asked where was he going. "There, Mother," he said, and pointed.

"You have a family?" she said. "And no pass papers?" It seemed something ordinary. He nodded. "Thari has a ladder," the woman said. "Let us go."

There were a few huts. He sat down on the edge and waited. He hoped someone would give him food, but it was not yet the time for cooking. But he was given water to drink in a half-gourd, brownish with earth, but water, the life restorer. He drank and the sweat started out on him. Then he waited, feeling it cool inside him, and drank again. An old man with few teeth, smoking a pipe with a foul smell, came out of a small round house; there was a ladder leaning against the wall. He told Petrus to carry it, then asked where he was going.

"There is no road," the old man said, "but it is not so far. See, past the fence, between the rocks and up. The track will take you onto the road. But you will not get to the track at once. No. But all will be well, my son."

They got to the fence, listened for hoofs. "They are far," said the old man. From the top, Petrus leapt down beside his bundle and thanked the old man. "Stay well, Father," he said.

"Go well, my child," the old man said and smiled, and shouldered the ladder.

It was all rocks, dust and dry thorny bushes. But he had drunk well. There was a kind of cattle track between the hills, winding in and out of great brown stones. He followed it, going up and up till he was out of sight of the border. Then he sat down on a stone and ate the rest of the bread and corned beef—if he kept it any longer it would go bad. He wished he still had the apple. Now his food was all finished. But he was in Bechuanaland. He patted the stone he was sitting on. And then he noticed the small hoof marks in the dust and wondered what they were, so small beside the big hoofs of the cattle, different from goats. When he saw the ones who had made the hoof prints, he was so surprised he just stood still with his mouth open. For a herd of impala exploded around him out of the bush, light and lovely, some suddenly spurting high up with arched backs like a sudden spray of water.

After a while, he had passed the hills and was in flat

country, bitterly dry; the track was fairly definite. It came out onto a road, not a metaled road, a road made of rutted and impacted dust. He had followed the road and had even begun to think that it might be safe to signal to a truck if one came, when something happened. He saw and heard a police car. Perhaps it wasn't coming after him. Perhaps it was looking for a thief or a murderer. But it made Petrus turn off the road and run, run.

Afterwards he could not remember the rest of the day. Only that he had gone on running, his feet, harder now, scuffing in the hot dust. And then there was no path. He had stopped and said to himself that he had been a fool, he had better go back to the road. But he could not find the road. He had tried to see a big tree to walk toward, but when he got nearer there seemed to be too many trees, he could not tell which was his one. He walked and walked, and suddenly it was night. He slept for a little and then he heard some beast make a snarling echoing noise. He could not tell if it was near or far. But he managed to climb into a tree and sat there, clinging to a spiky branch, sometimes dozing a little but never enough to let go. Not till morning when he slid off and collapsed for a time into sleep. Then the sun was up, the heat beginning.

He remembered coming to a cattle post and there was nobody there but a very old man with sore eyes who did not seem to understand anything, but at last grudgingly gave him a tin mug of milk. There were flies in the milk, but Petrus gulped it and spat out the flies. Then he went on. There must have been another night but he could only remember darkness and fear. He tried to cheer himself up by thinking of ways in which he could hurt or kill Sampson, but somehow he could never find a way to get Sampson into his power. Always, always, Sampson was with the police.

He remembered coming to a marshy place and hoping for water, but there was nothing but mud and rushes except perhaps in the middle where some cows were standing flicking their tails at the flies. And he could not get there because of the deep mud. He remembered seeing three ostriches walking with high steps among the bushes and they seemed to be much bigger than he had thought ostriches could be. And he walked and walked, but now he was walking more slowly and he could see no end to it. None.

And then he heard a noise that was utterly different from the noise of the bush, the sound of a train clonking and rattling slowly along, not near but giving a direction. Trains need water. He must get there.

But it was a long way to the railway line, with the thorns dragging at him and the dust and sharp grit working into him all the time. The line was fenced off and he walked along the fence for a while. Then he came to another fence, a farm, and the first thing he saw there was water, water slopping out of a trough. He couldn't get his eyes off it. He heard the chug of a pumping engine and the noise of stock moving. Could he slip under the fence and get at the water? He saw an African in blue overalls in the distance, and then, suddenly, saw the white farmer, a man with stubbly gray hair and steel spectacles, also in overalls. He walked over to the fence slowly, and Petrus was torn between fear of him and longing for the water. "Thirsty?" said the farmer, speaking in Tswana. "Come in, young man." And he pulled up the lower wire. Is it a trap? Petrus asked himself. But why should it be? He slipped in and stood eyeing the farmer, who pointed to the trough and at the same time seemed to be looking right through him. Petrus knelt and drank and then dared to scoop out a little water and wash his face. He turned to see if he had done wrong, but the man said, "Go on, wash. Plenty of water. Been in the bush, eh? You understand English?"

"Yes, baas, yes!" said Petrus. This was a white man speaking, not Afrikaans, but English, this English that Joseph had taught him, that they had spoken together. He undid the bundle and took out the piece of soap. The farmer lit a pipe and sucked at it. It was wonderful to be clean again, to have water between his toes; he dared to take off his shirt and wash some more.

"Better wash that shirt while you're at it," said the farmer. And this was a most extraordinary thing to say, for it seemed that the farmer was regarding him as a

111

person. It came into the tone of the voice, something new, altogether new from a white.

He washed the shirt and hung it over a bush and then, when he felt like himself again, he stood straight and said, "You let me do one day's work for my food, baas. Anything."

The man sucked at his pipe and didn't answer. After a while he said, in English, "Where are you bound?"

Was it safe to say? Petrus looked deep at the farmer and thought, yes it is safe, and whispered, "Mochudi."

"Got friends there?" Petrus nodded. The farmer took another puff, then said, "You from the other side?"

Petrus gave the ghost of a nod. "No papers, eh? And what do you think you'll get at Mochudi?"

Could he say? Yes, perhaps. "Education," he breathed.

"Those schools of theirs are pretty well crammed as it is," said the farmer. "Still—they might squeeze you in. Got any money?"

"For that only," said Petrus.

"Righty-o," said the farmer and suddenly called to the African, who came over lightly. "This boy's to work for you today, John. Set him to clean out the poultry house. You got any *ting* left?" The Motswana grinned. "You give him enough to keep his guts from squeaking till suppertime." He turned away.

John, the boss boy, signed to Petrus to come along, and there, at the back of the shelter, was a wooden porridge bowl half full of ting, the sour brown porridge made of millet that Bechuanaland people like so much, ever so much, more than mealie meal. "Eat," he said, and Petrus ate till he felt giddy, scooping it out with his fingers.

Now he had plenty of heart for cleaning out the chicken house, though he did not like the smell of chickens. He asked John about his baas, but John laughed and said there was nothing wrong there. Yes, he knew Mochudi, who didn't, but he was not a Mokgatla, he was a Mokwena. "My tribe and your tribe, we used to fight," he said, "but now we beat you at

113

soccer." They had stew later on that day with big pieces of meat in it, the kind you wouldn't be ashamed to give to a guest. Petrus tried to make it out, asked questions. The baas was English not Afrikaner, had been there for a long time. "Everyone knows him, everyone likes him. He is not different from us. We have that kind in Bechuanaland."

After the stew his eyes were dropping. He could not keep awake, not anyhow. He felt someone pick him up and carry him. But that was the last till he woke the next morning in a big rondavel with the men around him getting to their feet, laughing, talking, whistling. He worked with them all the next day, and ate with them. Once the white farmer went by, said something cheerful. Petrus listened in case anyone should speak of what had happened—over there. But nobody did and he dared not speak of it himself. Not yet.

In the evening the baas called him, took him down to the main road, past the railway. He leaned against the gate and watched the trucks, he seemed to know them all. "Not him, he's going to Mahalapye." "That man, he's a no-good, drove into my fence one day."

And at last, "There now, he'll take you." He signaled to the truck, which stopped, and leaned into the cab, talking to the African driver, both of them laughing together. Then he turned to Petrus: "You get in with him, young man. He'll take you to Mochudi. He'll show you where the Chief's place is. You'll be all right." And the queer thing was that Petrus felt that in some way he really meant it. He, a white, cared about him, an African.

So now there was Petrus with four meals inside him and a long sleep, washed, almost easy in his mind, on the way to Mochudi and knowing already that Bechuanaland was different. The road went up and down, always deep in dust; once they passed a tractor pulling along a great bundle of bushes to smooth out the dust ridges. Now it was unfenced but he could see fields on either side. The crops were poor, all the same. The driver was talking about the need for rain. It was another bad year. But when did they have a good year last? Oh, years back! Always, always, poor rains, no follow-up, plenty of people hadn't even sowed, hadn't the heart to plow. "So we stay poor, poor! You in the Republic, you get all the rain!" For a moment the driver seemed angry with him. Then, "You want to see the Chief?"

"I want education," said Petrus. "Do I go to the Chief for that?" It did not seem quite right and yet the white farmer too had said so.

"You a Mokgatla, boy?" said the driver. "You are *Kgabo*. Yes. Very well then, you go to the Chief."

Now there were small, odd-shaped hills rising from the flatland, the road dipped by a railway bridge and a pool of stagnant water. Above, on the slope of the hill, there were thatched round huts, not brick houses with

115

tin roofs like the ones Petrus was used to. Was he going to live in a hut? Well, yes, he supposed so. Suddenly they swung off the main road and over a level crossing, then up on a long curve, and now there were many people about, for the day was beginning to cool down toward night. Some of the people hailed the driver with abuse and shouted news, and he answered back. There were more brick houses here, a store and yes, that surely must be a school!

The driver stopped at a café, under a tree, off-loaded a crate, had a violent argument that ended in much laughing, then drove on, the road getting worse and worse, past kraals and houses and trees, nothing in rows, all haphazard, any way at all, with low walls around most of the houses and people moving in and out, and beginning to light candles or oil lamps that flickered at the backs of windows and door frames. The driver of the truck stopped. "This is as far as I go," he said. "Follow the road on. It goes through a big white wall and that is Sethebong, that is the Chief's house. Wait and he will see you."

So now Petrus walked on, feeling between his toes the warm dust of Mochudi. Children ran past him across the road and stopped and stared at him. A team of oxen had just outspanned and were moving slowly into the kraal, the bells tinkling sweetly. There was the big house, the size of a white man's house, and other smaller ones. There were rocks and trees. He did not

116

want to push himself forward so he sat down beside his bundle and waited.

Nobody had said anything about this. His mother had said nothing. His big brother had only said that Chiefs were out of date, that freedom and justice were all. There seemed to be many children about. Were they the Chief's children? They wore nothing but string kilts or little belts, they were almost like savages! No, there was a boy with schoolbooks, properly dressed. Schoolbooks! The half-naked children ran and shouted. At last one of them came over and said, "Why do you wait? Do you want to see Chief?" Petrus said that was indeed what he wanted, but for a moment half wished he was back in the bush among the strange noises of beasts, anywhere except here.

There seemed to be several people waiting; he thought he must watch what they did. But he felt far from home. Now it was quite dark and the din of the grasshoppers rang in his ears. There were cantering hoofs in the night, riders dismounting, a horse whinnying. One of the waiting men moved, and Petrus watched how he half knelt, balanced on his haunches, but spoke without ceremony. Whatever was the matter seemed to be got through quickly. The Chief looked around, saw him, pointed. Petrus came forward, the bundle in his hand, and half knelt as the man had done. He could not see the face of this Chief, only that he was young and moved quickly. And that he spoke with sharpness and decision, using few words. The moment Petrus gave his name, this Chief knew who he was. He said, "Your brother is in prison. You know that? You will stay here."

"How long—how long sentence?" Petrus asked, and his voice quivered.

"Ten years," said the Chief, "but he will get to know that you are safe."

"Ten years—oh—"

"You have to be brave. Become a fighter like your brother. Who are your uncles here?"

"The name I have kept in my head is Molemi, sir. The uncles —I think my mother said Thotwe—"

"Good, I know. I think he is back from his lands today. What standard at school?"

"Standard Five."

"You are younger than some of our Standard Fives. We will talk to the head teacher. Now, can you stay on the back of my horse if I take you over?"

"I think so, sir," he answered. Somehow he knew he had to be brave.

"Let's go, then." The Chief shouted and someone resaddled his horse and brought it around. The Chief sprang into the saddle, leaned over and pulled Petrus up behind him. The bundle was handed up. "Hold on, man. That's right, hold to my belt. We'll find your people."

CHAPTER 8

Newcomer

PHETO WAS IN TROUBLE. He had stolen sweets from the store and been caught. Molemi was affronted and furious that this should have happened in their family. He beat Pheto with his belt, hard, till he yelled, and threatened to keep him away from school. Pheto had thought that Molemi was away at the lands but he had come back suddenly, sick of looking on at his crops withering; if he had not felt like that he would not have thrashed Pheto so hard.

Pheto went out and lay in the dust outside the lapa, sobbing a little. He knew he had done wrong, brought shame on the family, but surely not so wrong as that! In a little Dineo came out too and sat beside him in the moonlight. She didn't say anything, but it was nice having her there. Letsebe was chanting over the lessons he had learned at school that day. Pheto did not want to hear him; the beating had shaken the letters out of his head.

Then they looked up. There was a horse coming through the night. Dineo shouted over the wall and her father came hurrying out, barefoot and in his tattered trousers only. "Kgabo!" But Dineo and Pheto ran around the corner of the wall and hid; they were always a little frightened. This was Kgosi, the Chief. And the Chief, Kgabo, he was—what? Surely someone to fear!

A boy slipped from the back of the Chief's horse. Molemi had found and lighted a candle and shone it onto the boy, who looked scared, yes, he was shaking. "Who is it, Kgabo?" Molemi said.

"This is your grandmother's grandson from the Transvaal. He is also a far cousin of your wife. Be good to him."

"The one whose teacher brother was sentenced to ten years and also—"

"*Khudu-thamaya!*" said the Chief sharply, and Molemi stopped in the middle of the sentence, for this is an old proverb about the tortoise which has many colors, but which color is a secret, and it means that a thing must above all not be told. For the Chief could see that Petrus could face the thought of his brother in prison, but most likely not of his brother being flogged

120

by the police. Time enough for him to know that when he was strengthened, fully one of the Tribe.

"Now, man," said the Chief to Petrus, "here is your home. I hope you will be able to go to school."

"I have money," said Petrus, very shyly.

"Listen to that, Molemi. Your son says he has money. He says too that he is in Standard Five. Take him to Segale school tomorrow and see the head teacher. No, this will be difficult. It is more than ten days after the beginning of term. Take him to the office; I will speak to Mr. Phirie myself."

"I have to go back to my lands, Chief."

"Then the boys will take him. But I shall come and see that he is looked after." And then the Chief wheeled the horse and it plunged and reared and suddenly went galloping off again into the night.

Petrus saw now that there were two boys watching him, both younger than he was, one without a shirt. He couldn't really see their faces and they said nothing. Behind one of them there was a smaller girl, thin and slender, a little girl in a string kilt, twisting her bare toes over one another. The man jerked his head at them: "Letsebe. Pheto," he said, and then, as an afterthought, "Dineo." Petrus spoke his own name, shakenly. They still stared.

Molemi shook his head like someone wondering what had hit him, then blew out the candle. The smell of it lingered for a while. But Petrus felt his hands being taken gently, and the two boys were guiding him into a corner of the house; they whispered and then spread a blanket on the floor. They went to sleep one at each side of him, but Petrus wondered why one of them turned and twisted and once woke in the night crying.

At early dawn he began to see the shape of the house, with Molemi moving about, knocking something over, muttering to himself. Then the little girl was moving, running out with a kettle, her feet making no sound. He looked about him, saw a battered wardrobe, some boxes and two rather broken chairs, some papers under a stone, one small lamp. What was it going to be like?

Molemi started back to his lands before it was wholly light, stalking off after his cups of tea, a cow-skin cloak over his shoulder, grumbling to himself, shouting at Pheto, threatening him with more and worse beatings. Petrus didn't know what to do. The boys hardly spoke to him, then Dineo said, "Come, you must greet Nkoko." She took him by the hand and led him to the other hut, where Nkoko was sitting on the ground, wearing her oldest, tattered blue apron, and making a *tlatla,* a wide basket without a handle, nicely patterned in gray and brown, the kind one carries on the head. She greeted Petrus formally, asking for news, first of his mother, then of members of his family whom he hadn't even heard of. But he heard now, for she told him all about them, and of things which they had done when they were boys and girls, long, long ago. He was

122

scared of Nkoko; he found her difficult to understand. He was glad when Dineo took his hand again and led him away. They had the remains of the tea, strong and cold with a pinch of sugar. Then Letsebe said, "Come," and started off.

"Where?" asked Pheto.

"To the office," Letsebe said.

It was quite a long walk, through this village or town with hundreds and thousands of houses, all put down simply where the people who intended to live in them thought would be nicest. Then a lapa was built around the house and plastered and there you were. Some had granaries like little huts on stick legs. But this year the granaries were empty. Many houses had shade trees planted around them. There was a pond, shrunken against a high dam wall, the water green and filthy. "When it rains," said Letsebe, "it becomes good again."

There were small kraals for cattle or goats, those that were kept in the town. The path wandered through and Petrus could feel people staring at him and speaking about him. There were low hills that cut the spread of the tribal town into smaller villages, wards under their own headmen. It seemed very strange to Petrus, out of all sense. Could he ever learn to live here? Then they were on a bigger road, dust and ruts and people, an ox team of sixteen oxen pulling a slow, long, creaking wagon with big wheels. And there at last was the office, a square, tin-roofed building with men going busily in and out or standing around, talking, waiting for something to happen. This was at one side of the kgotla square, at the other was a deep shelter of heavy branches. It was still early. Then there were hoofs, a rider clattering up, dismounting, and Petrus could see the face of the one whom, he supposed in a bewildered kind of way, was now his Chief, and it was a much younger face than he had guessed, creased into laughter.

"Chief has a car," said Letsebe disapprovingly, "he need not ride that horse. It is a wild horse; it kicks. But perhaps the car is broken again." He took Petrus around to a side door and showed him into a small office, cluttered with filing cabinets, parcels of books and school equipment, every kind of thing, and only just room to get around the desk in the middle with the typewriter and the neat piles of papers and forms. There was someone sitting there who looked over his spectacles at Petrus. He had graying hair, a thin, very kind face, and wore neat suspenders over a khaki shirt. "That is Mr. Phirie," said Letsebe. "Speak."

Petrus did not know whether to speak in English or in Setswana, but felt that this was an official occasion so perhaps it should be English. He explained who he was. Mr. Phirie put his fingertips together and listened. He had already heard this from the Chief, who had come early to the office. There were certain rules and regulations about childern going to school. They could not simply walk into a school and enroll with the headmaster so long after beginning of term. Mr. Phirie above all disliked breaking such rules, which were made for sensible and orderly conduct. Indeed, he himself had thought that the boy should wait. Perhaps, for example, he would not want to stay in Mochudi; one must see. But Chief had said this was a special case, a very special case. So he must consider carefully what should be done, and while the boy was speaking he must be watched with great attention. "I have money for education," said Petrus. "I was hoping too much—"

"Perhaps you should go to Isang School," said Mr. Phirie. "Standard Five. Let me see. But Isang is far from your house. And your cousins go to Segale School." He began to consult lists. Then, "Does the Chief know?"

"Yes," said Petrus. "It was he who sent me to you."

"That is how I brought him," said Letsebe. "Chief said."

Mr. Phirie seemed relieved; they too knew; the boy must mean it. He bent over his desk and ran his pencil down a list. "Yes," he said, "I shall send you to Isang." He looked up and smiled. "You will pay me for books, and pay your school fees there. That will be eleven rands and fifty-five cents exactly. I will give you a letter to the headmaster." He wrote it while Petrus carefully undid the stitches his mother had made, fastening the money inside his shorts. He wondered if he could make the stitches again. Perhaps someone would have a needle. Putting into his other hand the school fee money, he handed over what was needed for books, took and looked at them. Oh, there was almost the same arithmetic book! At least there might be somewhere among all this strangeness where he could find his way. "Now take him up to Isang," Mr. Phirie said to Letsebe. By now there were nearly a dozen or more children or grown-ups waiting at the entrance to the office.

"Let's go," said Letsebe, and led him around the back of the office and past three or four rondavels, round, thatched houses inside courtyards, then up a steep, rather smelly path between rocks and stones from which you could see farther and farther out over Mochudi. At the top there was a cleared space, a whitewashed school with high gables, a few remains of houses, thick bush at one side, and at the other a clear drop over the sheer rock, and a view out over another part of Mochudi, the winding riverbed with the green trees, cattle kraals, lands, far off the railway—you could tell because there was a puff of smoke moving slowly along it. And beyond a rise of hills, but always the far, open, unfenced country of Bechuanaland.

So what would it be like? Petrus was interviewed, paid his school fee and was put into the back of a class. There were boys dressed as he was, in shorts and shirt, girls in gym tunics; but most of them were older than he was, some much older. During recess there were questions, sometimes half shouted at him in the Sekgatla accent which he found a little hard to follow. He said he was from the Republic but he was a Mokgatla. He said nothing about his brother; if one of them had made any kind of scornful remark, he knew he must fight or scream with pain. One of the big boys dared him to jump between two huge rocks but he just managed it. Two of the big girls said something about him to one another which made him feel embarrassed. Then they all laughed. But a first day at school is always difficult. Petrus thought that at least he was up to standard, though some of the lessons went differently. Anyhow it was education. What he had intended to get.

In the afternoon he found his way back to Molemi's house, but he had to ask several times. The house was empty, for the others had their school in the afternoon.

There was nothing to eat, no water even. But he was tired, he just lay down in the shade of the house and slept, his head on his schoolbooks. He woke when Dineo brought him a bowl of porridge. He scooped it out and ate it hungrily though it had been made too quickly and he did not like it much. There was an old beer can with goat's milk in it, to go with the porridge; how different from his mother's pink and blue plastic! They were short of water that day. He offered to go with Dineo to fetch more water, but no, she said, she had brought what was due to them that morning. The borehole was not going well. Perhaps it was the engine but it seemed as if the whole land was thirsty. Besides, her father had drunk three cups of tea that morning, and Nkoko had spilled some; her hands trembled a little now that she was getting old and she had gone on too long working on the basket.

So it went that week. They had porridge every day and a little milk, and once Letsebe took down some bits of biltong from a string where they were hanging. They were black and salt and hard, strips of eland meat. One could nibble off the crisp edges, gradually getting a mouthful of meat. The children were all beginning to talk to one another now, but it made things difficult that Petrus, though not much bigger than Letsebe, should already be at the other school with only two years before secondary school, instead of what seemed like a lifetime.

Petrus thought he ought to try and help them with their homework. Letsebe wanted to be helped, but Pheto wasn't so sure. And Dineo had to do so much of the cooking and sweeping, both for them and for Nkoko, that sometimes she seemed to lose heart, although she had so much wanted to learn.

And then it was Friday. When the others came back from school there was no cooking, only a quick drink of goat's milk. The boys and Dineo took off their school clothes. Nkoko came hobbling over, yes, she would wash and press them. Yes, and Petrus must give her his shirt. Why should he wear a shirt at the lands? He took it off, puzzled, but glad to have it washed. "Are you ready?" said Letsebe. "We go now."

"But where?" asked Petrus.

"It is Friday," said Pheto. "We go to the lands."

CHAPTER 9

At the Lands

THEY WALKED AND WALKED. Why? What was happening? Petrus just hadn't understood yet that in the growing season, or what should be the growing season if there was rain, almost everyone in Mochudi goes out to the lands. He was hungry and kept on stopping to take thorns out of his feet. A wooden sledge crossed the path, drawn by six donkeys. It was loaded with two or three sacks and more than two or three large ladies singing hymns. Petrus had never seen a sledge being used, though they are practical enough in deep soft dust and can go where a car would stick hopelessly and even a wagon wheel would dig itself in. It seemed to him just silly. "Donkeys pulling donkeys!" he said. Dineo giggled.

But Letsebe was angry. "One of those is your aunt," he said. "If I tell her you said she was a donkey, she will tell her regiment and they will all come and they will beat you till you squeak for days!"

"That wouldn't matter," said Pheto, "but if they were angry with you, they might be angry with us too!"

Petrus said anxiously that he hadn't meant to insult anybody, but Letsebe went on being angry. Then Petrus got angry himself. He began to say exactly what he thought about a lot of things, about the dust and the dirt, no school toilets at Isang School, about the Sekgatla accent, about the stupidity of walking out to the lands every week! The other two boys only walked quicker. They seemed not to mind about thorns and stones, but Petrus's feet, though they were harder now, were not as tough as theirs.

After a bit he whispered to Dineo, asking about their aunt's regiment; again, he hadn't understood. Dineo said that all older people belonged to a regiment and if you said something disrespectful about one, you said it about all. But what exactly was a regiment? He remembered his mother had told him about them, because it was something that all Bakgatla knew; but he had paid no attention, not then. "They are given a name," said Dineo, "and their own songs. Our father has his songs. Our mother has her songs. A grown person will not sing children's songs. But we have many, we who are children. Our own songs. I have made a new skipping song. I will sing it to you." And so she did, pretending to skip with a rope as she went along, her voice tinkling like a little bell. Her brothers were scornful of her song, but Petrus liked it, though he could not make out all the words. He began to sing it with her, but she stopped him. "It is a girls' song!" she said. "You cannot sing it!"

It was all so difficult, and they went on walking. Sometimes they saw people but mostly not. It was long after dark when they got to the lands, suddenly turning in through a gap in a palisade toward firelight and the smell of cooking. Two women came to meet them— Tsholofelo and the other grandmother. They had heard about Petrus and greeted him warmly; he was almost too tired to answer as he should, and out of spirits with how the evening had gone. They seemed to sense this, left him, turned to the others. Tsholofelo ran her hands down their arms and legs. "Is Nkoko feeding you?"

"Yes, yes," they said, for they did get porridge every day and Nkoko put the meal into the pot while they were still at school, and if there was no meal it was Nkoko who went to the neighbors and borrowed a little. Some children did not even have a grandmother to help them but had to do everything themselves. They got very thin and sometimes they did not go to school. It could happen that a child alone like this could become ill and even die before anyone noticed. Yet most of them had some kind of relations to turn to if things got bad. It was only that sometimes nobody paid any attention to what was happening till perhaps it was too late.

Petrus slept late the next morning; the others were up and about, laughing, chasing the hens or one another. Dineo brought him a half-gourd full of cow's milk, sweet and fresh, still a little warm. But she only spoke to him in a whisper. Then she ran off. She was showing her other grandmother the letters she had learned, marking them with a stick in the dust. "Nkomeng was like this," said the grandmother to Tsholofelo, "perhaps we have another scholar." And oh, thought Dineo, shall I one day be as clever as Nkomeng, shall I go to the Molefi school? Shall I sit on the cool steps of the library and read books? Shall I have a gym tunic and shoes and a whole bottle of ink?

That wasn't a happy day for Petrus. He was out of everything. When Molemi and Letsebe went to the cattle post they didn't take him. He didn't yet clearly understand why some cows were at the lands, some at the cattle post. Nobody told him; he had to guess everything. He went off by himself and brought in wood for the women's fire and they looked pleased. But it was terrible to see the lands where there should have been broad waving leaves and beautiful brown tassels of millet, the mabele that is life for everyone. Now there was nothing but dry, thin stems and the leaves all torn and gray with heat. Only one corner had a few ears, not more than one or two bags. There had been a small burst of rain, but it had only touched half of one of Molemi's fields. There was no sweet cane this year, just a little patch of beans, hardly any squashes and watermelons. Tsholofelo stooped and tapped one of the melons, but it was not ripe yet. "Perhaps next week," she said.

The others all started playing games they knew, make-up games, mostly with the little ones. Petrus was left out, not knowing what to do. He was pleased when Dineo pounced on him and said, "You be the lead ox!" They were a team in a wagon, and little Moputso was driving them, pretending to crack a huge whip, and shouting. It might have been his own Rebecca and Luke.

But over at the cattle post Letsebe found he was

being shown things by his father that he would not have been shown before he went to school. So that school was one step up toward being a man. He had kept a sugar sweet for his little brother Thotwe, one of two which an uncle had given him on Friday; he had kept it carefully in its paper. Now he held Thotwe's hand and swung it while he sucked the sweet. But what was interesting was to listen to the men talking about cows. He went with his father to look at the cattle. How beautiful they were, what pride to see them! There is a different word in Setswana for an ox or a cow of every color and with every shape of horns or build of body. These were old words with much meaning; for centuries the Batswana had loved their cattle. It is only lately that they have had to think about making money out of them.

Every man at the cattle post had his own brand, and the beasts were branded on the flank. Now Letsebe understood that these marks were letters such as he had made at school. There was one ox in particular that was looking well, although there was so little grass and the beasts were mostly grazing on the leaves of bushes. "That is indeed a fine ox!" said Letsebe shyly, joining in with the men.

"And the government favoring the beasts from the north!" grumbled Molemi, for everyone in Bechuanaland thinks that someone else's cattle are fetching a better price than his own.

"Did you think of selling one, my father?" asked

Letsebe, low and respectfully. This was a serious matter, a matter for men.

"Perhaps," said Molemi, "if I can find a place on a truck and not have to pay too much for it." They looked again at the big ox. "Yes, that one. Perhaps Norman will have a place on his truck. I will speak to him. I will go to him at Mochudi. Yes, I will speak."

"Beautiful, too beautiful!" said Letsebe. One day he too would have cattle. How could one ever bear to part with one of them! And yet, that would be money. There seemed to be no other place for money to come from.

Thotwe pulled him away in a while to look at "his" ox, which he was now able to ride. Then Letsebe found his own riding ox, but it looked thin; nobody else had looked after it as he used to do before he went to school. But what could one do? Nothing.

The men at the cattle post talked almost wholly about cows; they talked about the look of the beasts at other cattle posts. Some of them thought it was worthwhile to get a good bull from the bull camp which the Tribe had established to bring in a better breed. Others said that it was not worth the money you paid. Again some said that if one was selling it would be best to sell soon; there was so little left for the beasts to eat, and it would get worse and worse for eight or nine months until the rains came—if they did come. But surely there must be a good year soon, a year to make up for all the bad ones! But others said no, they would not sell. The Government had told them to sell. Was that not proof that selling was wrong? The Government only wanted to rob you. That was what they said and stupidly went on saying and always would, even when they had Independence. Molemi sometimes agreed with them and sometimes not.

There was a bag full of sour milk at the cattle post; Letsebe had a bigger share than he used to have before he went to school. But still, he was only a boy, a listener on the edge of the talk. He would be a boy until he went for initiation and had a regiment of his own. But that was many years ahead. They started back in the late afternoon. Molemi had his gun and kept a watch for anything they could eat. They saw a big turkey bustard in a clearing, but too far for a shot, and running away. "I remember," said Molemi, "once when I was young, I shot a turkey bustard, a *kgori*, and I said to my friends, what shall we do? I had not gone to school yet, for in those days we did not go to school until we were sixteen or eighteen, big boys. Before that we herded. Those were better days."

Letsebe said respectfully, "Yes, my father." He was not sure if it would be better to wait and not go to school for another six years, but he could not say so.

"Well, we decided that we must take this kgori to the men of an older regiment, who were at the next cattle post. So we put it on to a stick and we walked and walked. It was ten miles, but we knew we were doing the thing that was right. And in the end we got there and we gave them the kgori and they were pleased. They said we had acted rightly and as was due to them. They gave us plenty of milk. Milk and praise: what is better? So we walked back and it was well."

"But if you had not taken it, my father?"

"Then, if they had heard, they would have thrashed us. And we would have deserved it. The young must always give respect to their elders. This you know."

"This I know, my father," said Letsebe. Dark was beginning to fall and still no game.

And then out of the bush in front of them a duiker flashed and jumped. Molemi lifted his gun, fired. The duiker fell over, kicked once or twice, died. They ran on, but it was a good shot; no need for a second. Now the duiker must be carried back. Molemi had a strip of leather hanging from his belt; he cut it in two. They tied the duiker's feet together and ran a pole through. Then they lifted and carried it. They still had five miles to go, but they were carrying food. It had been almost too dark for the shot, but the duiker had come just in time. And Molemi was a good shot. He sang a little as he carried and walked, and sometimes his feet moved in the beat and shuffle of a dance. And Letsebe felt that there was no father like his own.

Back at the hut in the lands, the women ran out to greet them. Then there was talk and praise and the duiker to be skinned and hung up but best of all, the liver to be taken out, cut up and roasted on the fire. There was enough for all. Maputso was asleep on a skin rug in the corner of the hut but Tsholofelo woke him up so that he could have a piece of liver to chew at, fresh, tender liver, so good!

After this supper, the other grandmother began to tell a story. It was a story they all knew but yet it was a good story to hear. It was about the time when all the animals went out to graze far off in the veld, and became thirsty. So the baboon went on ahead to drink at the waterhole, and the other animals came behind Mr. Tshwene, the baboon, last of all, Mr. Mmutle, the hare. Now they were all hurrying along when Mr. Tshwene saw the snake, Mr. Noga, and a stone had fallen onto his back so that he was pinned down. Mr. Noga, the snake, begged help of Mr. Tshwene, the baboon, and Mr. Tshwene lifted the stone and let it go. And then what happened? Snake says he is going to eat baboon!

So Mr. Tshwene, the baboon, called on all the other animals to help him as they passed by to drink. He was bringing his case to them to be judged—must he be eaten because he had helped? But all the other animals hurried by, for they were afraid. But last of all, at the end of the animals, came Mr. Mmutle, the hare, and he listened to what Mr. Tshwene told him: how he had unpinned the snake from the stone and now the snake was going to eat him. "Yes," said the snake, "I am going to eat Mr. Tshwene!" "How then, were you pinned down by that stone, Mr. Noga?" asked Mr. Mmutle, the hare. "May I not see?" Mr. Noga agreed, and let Mr. Tshwene put the stone back on him. "Are you now pinned down as you were, Mr. Noga?" said the hare, and the snake agreed that this was how it was. "Then let us two run away!" said hare to baboon, and Mr. Tshwene and Mr. Mmutle ran away hard, and the snake was left under the stone. So the snake died and the baboon was saved, all by the cleverness of the hare.

There were many, many stories like this, and the old people knew them, having heard them from those that were older still and were now dead. Some of these stories had songs in them, or the noises of animals. Everyone liked to hear them, even the older people who also read newspapers or, now that there was a little library in Mochudi, took books about motorcars or history or economics out of that library. None of this spoiled the old stories.

On Sunday the uncles came over and all greeted Petrus and asked him for news of his mother and all his other relations. They asked about his brother, saying how terrible it was to be imprisoned for so long and for so little. But he would come out, perhaps before the end of ten years, and be a teacher again. None of them spoke about the beating. They asked, too, how he himself had made the crossing. "Ah," said Thotwe, the lucky uncle, "it is well that you are a Mokgatla; now you have a place to come to. Others are not so fortunate." They asked

140

about his schooling and were pleased that he was at Isang. "This family is a clever family," said Thotwe.

"All clever," said Mooki, the unlucky uncle, and looked around for beer. Tsholofelo had brewed a small pot and brought it over; it was gray and thick, with a nice sour taste. One glass hurts nobody. But Mooki went on drinking it. Molemi was angry because he had not left enough for the rest of them and pushed him a little, but not much because he was older.

"I have a present from Nkomeng for this little one," said Uncle Thotwe suddenly, and he brought out a parcel, done up in newspaper. Inside it there was a gym tunic. "This she wore when she passed Primary Leaving Examination so well," said the uncle, "but now she is in Form III. Perhaps it will be lucky for Dineo."

Dineo was happy! Now she would be like the smartest girls at school! Surely her mother could find a white shirt to go under it. They held it up to her. It was too big, but the bottom could be turned up and it had a belt that would tie around. If she was careful, it would do her for a long time. And perhaps this meant that Nkomeng thought she too would get a first class in Primary Leaving and be able to go on!

There was talk about self-government and the promises of the political parties. Which would give the best prices for beef? But Thotwe thought also about health and education and above all water. He spoke about dams and how to keep the cattle from destroying

141

them. Petrus listened from the back, trying to find out more about Bechuanaland, this country that, he supposed, was his country now. But Mooki was asleep and snoring in the shade of the tree where the duiker had been hung before it was skinned and cut up.

Sometimes they talked about rain and crops. Rain. How they needed rain. But Molemi complained that in the old days there was always some crop if you plowed at the right time. "And so I do always," he said, "I plow when Selemela is there"—he pointed to the sky and the cluster of stars that are called Selemela—"and the Dogs are chasing the Pigs down to Selemela. I have always plowed then."

"It was so in the old days," said Mooki, his voice slurred with drink, "in the old days the Chief said, 'Now is the time to plow.' We got good crops."

"I do not think we always got good crops," said Thotwe in a voice of rebuke. "I think there were years which were as bad as this. But we do not remember them because we do not like to remember them."

And what, thought Petrus, was Selemela and the Pigs?[1] And then he began to remember that sometimes his mother used to call the stars by names which his teacher brother had said were old-fashioned. But here, so much was old-fashioned! It was good, all the same, that they had duiker meat to offer to the uncles. All of it

---

[1] In Europe we call the Dogs and the Pigs Orion's Sword and Belt. Selemela is the Pleiades.

was cooked, for meat would not keep in the heat, and some was wrapped in the newspaper that the gym tunic had come in, for the children to take back. Nkoko would be pleased; it was too long since she had eaten meat. None of them minded having that kind of extra weight on their heads during the walk back.

CHAPTER 10

Tribe and Chief

THE NEXT WEEK Petrus wrote to his mother. He had never written a real letter before, only the kind of letter one has to write in school: letter to an employer, letter thanking for Christmas gift. Not the letter of someone desperately wanting news, wanting love and touch, in a strange place, uncertain, unhappy. And suddenly he thought, If it is like this for me, how much worse for my brother! To feel as I feel, but not to be able to run or jump or even go to school—yes, he thought, or to have Dineo as a sister. And he added to his letter that he liked his sister Dineo. Yes, he said to himself, I like Dineo, I like duiker meat, most of the time I like school. Above all I like to look out from school, past the great rocks,

144

away across the river and the houses and the trees. When I look out I am like an eagle. And then he thought, But my mother was at Mochudi once. It must be many years ago, but she will remember Isang, high on the hill. It is the first thing one sees, almost, coming to Mochudi, the white steep roofs of Isang and the dark hill behind and below.

But he could not put it into words any more than he could put into words or clear thoughts any of what he felt about his brother. He should be picturing his brother shut in a little dark room, for ten years. But he could not do it. Not his brother Joseph, who was always arguing and singing and reading books and saying that things would be different soon, soon. He pictured to

himself his brother sprinting, showing the boys how to stand, how to get off the mark. And that was all over. Sampson had watched too, all the time waiting to betray, to shut the sprinter's legs up into a little room. Oh no, no. But he could not write, could never put on paper, how much he hated Sampson. That was all too deep. In the end he did not like the letter he sent to his mother. But it was the best he could do and he posted it, putting on one of the pretty Bechuanaland bird stamps, the two-and-a-half-cent one.

Coming back from Isang he usually went past the houses and the big tree by the Kgotla square, and sometimes there would be a case being heard in the Chief's court, or sometimes a tribal meeting when the whole space was crowded with men and even some women. At one side there was a deep shelter, a roof of dark branches held up by poles, with benches underneath; there were often some of the older men sitting there. Sometimes there was a table and a clerk taking notes, and on a low chair the young man who had ridden through the night with him, sitting in judgment: the Chief in Kgotla. Once or twice he waited to see what the case was about. It seemed as if there was always much talk, questions, discussions; the man accused would answer and argue. A grown man might be fined, perhaps in cattle; but young men who fought each other were usually caned. They didn't like it, but at least they weren't shamed by it. They didn't feel different afterwards, only a bit sore, and knowing quite well it would happen again if they did the same thing. And when they got up and shook themselves, other people didn't dodge them or pity them. It was taken for granted that they had accepted their punishment, they felt shame for the wrong which they had done and now it was over and they were back in the Tribe.

Doubtfully, Petrus supposed it was all right. For him, beating had always meant beating by a white man, a farmer flogging a man almost to death to frighten the others or because he enjoyed it: or a flogging in a police cell with the whites looking on, making their jokes. Petrus hadn't listened to his brother talking with friends for nothing. He had seen for himself how it was, hurrying past. A man came out from a police beating utterly shamed, deeply angry. He couldn't make a joke with a man who had beaten him, as they did here.

There was much said about beating. Once he had stayed on the edge of a big *pitso,* a tribal meeting, with hundreds and hundreds of men and women gathered in the Kgotla square. They spoke about a Parent-Teacher Association, using the English words. But so many of them thought that this would simply be a kind of committee to punish the bad boys and girls, the ones who stole, or dodged going to school, or were disrespectful to their elders. One man said that now all bad children would be taken to the Chief and he would cane them, and all seemed pleased at this.

But the Chief said again and again that it wouldn't be like this, that it was for teachers and parents to speak together quietly about the children, what kind of children they were, what they wanted to be when they were older, whether they wanted to be farmers or engineers, teachers or vets, whether they had special difficulties. The Chief looked rather strange and far away, wearing a dark suit, a collar and tie, as he walked through the men into his place under the Kgotla shelter and shade. He looked half like a young *moruti,* a preacher. And all the men who were wearing their ordinary torn or patched clothes, their big feet dusty, stood up and if they had hats they took them off and everyone said "Kgabo," low and deep and respectfully. For that is the tribal word of the Bakgatla and the Chief above all is Kgabo. But the women still sat on the ground, some with umbrellas and handbags. It was only lately that they had started coming to the meetings, but now they spoke out at them.

There was also talk about cattle, about the railway asking for the price of carrying a beast to market when it was put on the train. And people did not at all like this, although they had been told that they would get a better price in the end because the rail charge would not be taken off it. But still they did not or would not understand. It seemed to Petrus that this was like a shop not giving credit. But nobody seemed willing to think of it that way, though it was explained many times.

Petrus wondered sometimes if things would go differently when he and the others at school were grown up and able to come to the tribal meetings. He asked an older man when they would be old enough to come and this man said it would be after regimentation when they were truly men. And it suddenly came to Petrus that perhaps he too, when he was much older, might have to go out with a regiment and come back changed. How? And he was half afraid but half wondering greatly what it would be like.

He asked more. He asked about the sentences in Kgotla, in the Chief's court. Someone told him that the one sentenced could always appeal to the District Commissioner's court, the Government court, if he felt himself unjustly treated. "But a young man who likes life had better not do that," the man who was telling him said, and laughed. "Go to the D.C.'s court and they may put you in prison, perhaps for months. That is terrible. It goes on and on. Here at the Chief's court it is all over quick. If you ever get into trouble, young man, you will remember which to choose."

But Petrus didn't want to get into trouble. He wanted to learn, he wanted to get hold of all this world that lay inside the books. One day Nkomeng told him about the library and how, when you were in the second year of the secondary school, you could go in there and choose a book and read it, at your own pace. She could not explain, but it was different, reading a book like that,

149

perhaps sitting on one of the new library chairs, with books all around you.

"Would you like to read a book?" she asked Petrus. "A real book? I have some books at home. And our lamp is better." So that evening, Petrus went to the lucky uncle's house and Nkomeng showed him her books; some of them were picture paperbacks but some were real books like schoolbooks with shiny covers. He picked one up. It was called *Robinson Crusoe,* but he could not understand it because of the sea; one heard about this sea in books, but could it be real? There were some very long words too. He picked up another, about a cowboy, and that seemed better because it was about cows and cows were real. And then he found a geography book, and that was much better because it was about the kind of things they had in class; it was a helping book that might show him things to write in his next composition. He had not understood at all about winds, but this book made him see. In a while Nkomeng brought him in half a Coke and laughed. She said, "You will like the library when you are no longer a child and can go there. Have you been to the community center?"

"I have," said Petrus doubtfully.

"I know," said Nkomeng, "you have stood outside and watched at dances. You have stood outside and listened at concerts. You must come in. There, you could read. There are papers. Papers with pictures. Petrus, do you know at all what is happening outside

Mochudi?" He shook his head. "But you must know. It is not enough to read the bit of newspaper something is wrapped in. Here is Bechuanaland we are having self-government. Have you not heard the trucks going around and the loud voices out of the machines?"

"The Domkrag trucks?"

"Yes, the People's Party trucks too. Is your father registered? Does he have that card that makes him able to vote? And your mother?"

"He said once he had the card but he did not know how to vote. Chief has not said."

"Chief will not say. He has told them that. He has told them loud. It is for them to say. To use their minds. When I am able to have a vote I will think hard by myself and then I will vote the right way. Now, Petrus, you will come to the center. I will show you how to read the papers, I will show you what you may touch yourself. All helped to build the center. All carried bricks. I carried bricks myself. Tell me you will come there."

So Petrus said, yes, he would. But he did not go at once. Partly he did not want at once to do what a girl had told him to do. And he did not want anyone to laugh at him. And partly because in the evenings there was always something to do. Mochudi was quiet in the hot afternoons. It was as though the heat of the sun wanted to beat you down and kill you. Better to stay in the shade, sleep through the bad time if you could. And again, it was quieter because a thousand of the smaller children were at the primary schools, while the older ones who had already been to school slept or read their lessons over or did their arithmetic. But at Molefi, the secondary school, lessons went on all day with the same children, and they had their dinner at school.

But this arrangement of shifts at the primary schools was changed around from time to time, and often this was not done by the teachers, but was carefully thought out by the children, to make easier walking for the ones who lived far out. Then the morning children would come in the afternoon instead, and the afternoon children in the morning.

Then after all the schools were shut, the sun began to drop and the heat began to drain out of the golden air, and people stirred themselves. By the time the come-to-supper star was showing, those who had food cooked it. Others did without, or perhaps had a cup of tea. Then the town became full of sounds, some near and some far off. There was the sound of a wagon being outspanned, the shouting, the dropping of the chains, the bell of the lead ox going back into the kraal. There were goats and sheep bleating, dogs barking, cocks crowing, the bray of a donkey or the whinny of a horse. But mostly it was people, the people of the Kgatla singing, shouting, talking loudly and cheerfully to one another, visiting, in and out of houses and lapas, talking things over,

152

spreading the news or making it sound more interesting than it was.

On a fine evening the children all came out and played, especially under certain big trees or in stretches of grass—or what should have been grass, but in a bad year was mostly sand. They played more on moonlight nights because then they felt safe—they could see that there weren't snakes or scorpions about. All the smaller children played together; they had taken off their school clothes and were almost as naked as the night. There was no thought about whose parents were rich and whose poor; if a child had sweets, they would be shared. They played running and hiding and clapping games; they played skipping games, making up the rhymes, making skipping patterns. Sometimes they played weddings, and then it was all done according to the proper form, with the boy's make-believe uncles going to visit the girl's make-believe parents, to ask for her hand in marriage. There would be running from one ward of Mochudi to another, serious playacting by both the "families" and in the end a wedding procession with the bride all dressed up with a veil, escorted by all her friends.

But on cloudy nights or nights with only a little moon, children stayed inside the lapas, around the stick fires. That was the time for storytelling, for singing old songs and making up new ones to the same tune. People

153

mostly gathered in groups; sometimes some of the relations came to see Nkoko, and sometimes the children all wandered off. Letsebe and Pheto had made up with Petrus; it was all forgotten. Next weekend when they went out to the lands, there was one ripe watermelon. They all shared it, crisp and sweet and sun warm, thirst quenching; they spat out the black seeds and the hens clucked around, picking them up. "Next year," said Letsebe consolingly, "there will be many, many melons."

"If God is good to us," said Tsholofelo.

"I could eat three melons," said Pheto, "and sweet cane. Three sticks of sweet cane I could eat. There is no sweet cane this year."

"Next year," said Letsebe again. And how could the Bakgatla, how could any of the Batswana, have gone on living without this hope, this almost certainty that next year things would be better?

Pheto was making himself a banjo with an old tin as a sounding box; he spent hours and hours over it and in the end it sounded wonderfully sweet and nice. He knew dozens of tunes, some old and some new. Petrus knew some that he didn't know, hummed them to him and in a few minutes he had picked them up. Now and then a band would come to Mochudi and play Twist for a whole evening. Then everyone would dance. They didn't have to think how to do it: somehow it was the natural way of dancing. As soon as a baby started walking he would begin wriggling fat legs Twist-fashion, the moment there was a scrap of Twist music anywhere.

Most African people have drums, but not the Batswana. However, everyone likes them in a band, and sometimes they beat time on cans or petrol drums. All the school children did the Twist, moving as supply as bits of rubber. Sometimes there was a dance at the community center. Those that paid to get in danced in the hall, but the rest danced outside on the hard, dusty ground, for Twist doesn't need a dance floor. The white light of the lamps inside made patches of brightness;

the thump of the jazz was almost as clear. But one night the dancers outside were suddenly all scattered by a galloping horse, and there was the Chief, lifting his whip and leaning over to beat a dancer over the shoulders. "Those who dance, must pay!" he said and his face was angry. "It is your hall, you must help it!" And then he said, "And schoolchildren must get to bed in good time or they will sleep all through school the next day!"

Petrus, hiding behind a corner of the building, saw Chief's face, which he had only known kind or composed, in this mask of anger, and he wished it would change back. He did not want to be afraid of the Chief, yet now he had to be. But it was partly his fault, though he had done no worse than the others.

Chief went into the hall of the center, paying to go in, and Petrus saw through the window that he was dancing lightly and with full rhythm. He danced with two or three girls, among them Nkomeng, and his face began to change back to the smiling face. Petrus was glad.

Sometimes Chief came to watch the football; the boys liked that. There was a young white boy called Simon who taught them soccer; they were pleased to be taught, though it was work to remember the rules of this game. He taught them relay racing and jumping; those who did best would go with Simon to do all these things against other schools. Nkomeng was on one of the girls' teams wearing a pair of borrowed boys' shorts. Petrus clapped when she did well, for now they were the same family. But sometimes, watching, he suddenly couldn't bear it. He almost hated Simon, the friendly white boy, because it was he who was coaching them and not Joseph.

Once, when he was standing at the edge of the sports field looking on, he had tried to speak of this to Nkomeng. She nodded; but had she understood? And then he said, "One day at least I will kill that Sampson, the one who betrayed my brother. I will kill him dead."

Nkomeng hesitated and then she said, "I can see that if I were a man I would want to kill my enemies. That kind of enemy. But—"

"But what?" said Petrus angrily.

"But you can do more for your brother if you get education. If when he comes out of prison he sees you as a teacher, here in Bechuanaland where you can teach as a freeman, or perhaps as a doctor. A doctor can do much good for Africa. Would that not be even better than the death of his enemy?"

Petrus did not answer. She was only a girl. He did not want the killing of Sampson taken away from him. But in a while, as the words came back into his mind, he began to think that, after all, she could be right.

After a while Petrus began to fall into the life of Mochudi. Before the elections he listened at the edge of meetings, big, long meetings with many questions, that were allowed and encouraged, where people said everything they liked! Meetings of Africans. In the Republic of South Africa a meeting of only three or four people would have meant police and prison. But here—this must indeed be freedom.

On election day he watched the long, orderly, slow-moving queue of men and women, all in their best, clutching their registration cards, going to vote for the first time. In the end Molemi and Tsholofelo had gone to vote with the rest, even though Kgosi still had not told them which way to vote. But it was an occasion. It was like New Year.

And now Petrus began to help his new father and uncles with men's things. Once his uncle Thotwe called him in the middle of the night when he was asleep, to come and help with the inspanning of the wagon that was to take him and some others out to the cattle post. It was a long journey to the uncle's cattle post, more than thirty miles, and better to do it in the cool of the night. This was a night with a full moon, as easy to see in as daylight, almost. There were half a dozen men at the kraal, but Uncle Mooki was too drunk to be much use except to be funny for the others. There was the big wagon; he could see there were sacks in it and branding irons and some wire. In front of it the chain was spread and the double yokes, each one a wooden beam with four wooden pegs driven through it, two for each ox. The oxen were being taken out of the kraal; riems of dry hide, narrow strips stronger than rope, were put around their necks. They were stood in a row and everyone began to count them, to see that there were eighteen— nine span of them. The oxen sometimes backed out or plunged, and some of the men were not very good at counting. Petrus held one of the oxen. It was a good ox, pleasantly spotted; he felt he was beginning to know a little about oxen.

Then Thotwe shouted and all ran forward with their oxen, onto the chain. Petrus helped to lift the beam of the yoke and knot the riem around the peg and the neck of his ox. The oxen understood and stayed quiet. Everyone shouted and told old jokes. Uncle Mooki fell over the chain. Then all had their yokes fast, but still Petrus could not see what would happen; he thought they must move slowly to get disentangled. But suddenly Thotwe cracked the long whip, high in the moonlight, over the oxen. And then the lead oxen plunged forward at a run, then the next span, and the next and the next, and suddenly they were all bounding forward, the chain running free, and the cart bumping after them, its big wheels jumping rocks and ridges. Everyone ran after it. Thotwe suddenly called to Petrus: "Coming? To the cattle post?"

Petrus hesitated. "School?" he said.

It was a Thursday evening. "One day!" his uncle shouted at him. "Come with the men!"

So he jumped onto the moving wagon and off they

went under moon and stars, first through the sleeping town—though they shouted into plenty of houses and men staggered to the door, blinking, to see what was on—and then onto the road, but soon turning off onto a bush track. Lying in the wagon on the sacks, listening to

the men talking, Petrus could sometimes see far through openings in the bush and sometimes the trees almost met overhead and the night was as dark as though it had been inside a house. And then again they would be out under the wide night with the Milky Way, cradle of lightnings, so unthinkably high above them. Once they heard a growling and the oxen swerved nervously. Someone fired and whatever it was slunk off.

And all the time he was listening to the talk of the men and knew he could understand it in a way he could not have done a few weeks earlier. He could see why some things were serious and others not, and it was different from the things that were taken seriously in the Republic. He could tell that often they were going back to something in history, using a word or a phrase with a big and proud meaning. I do not know the meanings yet, thought Petrus, I can only guess at them, but some day I shall know. Some day I shall be truly one of the Bakgatla. And so he slept under the stars in the rocking ox wagon.

It was good at the cattle post: fresh milk and sour milk, meat. And much talk and disputes that sounded fierce and furious but ended in laughter. And sometimes a few dance steps but not Twist, something nearer war, something in the world of men. Petrus had a letter from his mother in the pocket of his shirt, but it had not said much to him. Next time, she wrote in her letter, she would try to send money, two or three shillings, but things were difficult still. She did not tell him what she was working at but wrote about the family. He liked to hear about Rebecca and Luke but the neighbors had faded a little. And perhaps his mother was no better at writing letters than he was himself. And she said nothing about his brother, nothing at all. Perhaps there was nothing to say. She had heard nothing. She had not been allowed to see him; perhaps she did not know where he was, which prison. It was a way they had of hurting people. The ones outside. And the ones in. A man went to prison and even the thoughts of those he had left, even their love, could not reach him. His brother was in prison, far from the laughter of the cattle post, that was real. And this was real, all these men with whom he belonged, among whom he was growing up: his tribe.

CHAPTER 11

Rain

NKOKO WAS TELLING Dineo a story. This was a reward, because Dineo had at last made a clay pot that satisfied her grandmother, a nice-shaped clay pot with a lip, the shape of clay pot that Kgatla women have always made. Dineo had built it up with coils of clay, rubbed between her hands, and then smoothed and smoothed, very carefully. Pheto had come and looked at her as she worked, saying nothing; then he had brought over a piece of white marula wood that he had broken off at the bottom of a branch. He was working at it with a knife and already it was taking the shape of something, perhaps a dog. He sat at the edge of the step where he too could hear the story.

Nkoko pointed to her hens, and there was one of them asleep in the shade, its leg tucked up under its wing.

"Once upon a time," she said, "the jackal used to come and eat the hens. And the cock wondered what to do. But he did not know. So one day the jackal was coming and he saw the cock standing on one leg with the other leg tucked under his wing, and he said, 'Man, where is your other leg?' 'Oh,' said the cock, 'I have taken it off and taken it to the smith to be made stronger.' So the jackal went off and he told the rest of the jackals.

"Well, then, another morning, along came the jackal, and he found Mr. Kgogo, the cock, standing on his two legs but with his head under his wing. So the jackal said, 'But, Mr. Kgogo, where is your head?' The cock spoke from under his feathers, saying, 'My leg has come back

from the smith's as you see. But my head was not strong. So I have sent my head there to be made better.' And the jackal looked at the leg and it seemed to be large and strong and handsome, so he went back to the jackal people and told them of the things he had seen.

"So, two days later he went visiting again, and there was Mr. Kgogo wearing his head again, and the comb seemed to be large and shining and beautiful. So all the jackal people came to see this extraordinary thing and they all listened; they sat on the ground like dogs with their tongues hanging out while Mr. Kgogo, the cock, told them about the wonderful smith.

"Well then, a day came when the jackal had a headache. He came to the cock and said, 'Take my head to the smith, for it aches.'

"'Certainly I will do this for you, man,' said Mr. Kgogo, 'just put your head down on that block of wood.' So that was just what the jackal did. Mr. Kgogo took an ax and cut off the jackal's head, so that the jackal died altogether. Then the fowl cut the jackal up into little bits, put him in the pot and ate him.

"Now this was the day when Mr. Mmutle, the hare, dropped in to visit Mr. Kgogo, who offered him some of the mince. 'What kind of meat is this?' said Mr. Mmutle. 'It is the chief jackal,' said Mr. Kgogo, 'but do not tell the others. Only tell them that they have head-worms and perhaps they will all come my way.' And he explained his plan to Mr. Mmutle.

"So when the other jackal people asked Mr. Mmutle, the hare, what had happened to the chief jackal, Mr. Mmutle looked wise and said that they should all move into colder country where they would get well from the head-worms which had come into their heads and which had killed the jackal leader. Well, they went away to a colder place, but there was frost and their heads ached more; they did not know what to do, for they thought it was an order that they should stay there. But at last it became too much and they went back one by one, their tails drooping, and said to Mr. Mmutle, 'What shall we do? Do we still have these worms in our heads?'

" 'Yes,' he said, 'you have indeed, and your only hope is to go to Mr. Kgogo and beg him to cut off your heads and send them to his friend, the smith, to be melted down and made well.' So they came to Mr. Kgogo, the cock, and he agreed to cut off their heads and send them to the smith, but they must come one by one. So that was what they did, and in this way Mr. Kgogo cut off the heads of every one of the poor jackal people and that was the end of them."

Nkoko stopped and looked at the children. "This was so," said Dineo, satisfied, stretching herself, stretching her toes and her fingers.

"This was so," her grandmother said.

"This was not so," Pheto murmured to himself, but

166

not loud enough for Nkoko to hear. The dog he was making was already a little like a dog. It had big floppy ears like a wood-dog, like one of the Chief's golden-colored hounds that went with him when he was out hunting. Its legs were not so long but they ended in the dog's paws. Once Pheto had been sent with a message to Sethebong, the Chief's place, and there was Chief Linchwe running his hands over the dogs and pulling ticks out of them. The dogs wagged their tails and when Chief pushed them away, they came back to him, smiling with their dog faces, especially the dog called Domkrag, who put up its feet on him; he remembered the shape of the dog's paws. He looked up. "There is Petrus," he said.

Petrus came over, walking a little stiffly, and greeted his grandmother. All the people who speak Setswana are always greeting one another, even if they have met already that day. It is polite. Above all, young people must be polite to older ones. Dineo got up and stirred the porridge in the pot with a big wooden spoon. Pheto showed Petrus the dog he was making. He was afraid for a moment that Petrus would not like it, or perhaps he might think it was not a dog but a wild animal or even a donkey. However, Petrus saw at once that it was a dog and praised it as they walked back across the lapa. Nkoko called after them, "See the clouds! There will be rain."

167

Pheto walked close to Petrus. He whispered, "Who did it? Was it the headmaster?" Petrus nodded. "How many?"

"Five," said Petrus casually, "and he hits hard. But now I have forgotten it. If our uncle wants me, I shall go again to the cattle post. I can always learn harder at school the next day. It will not stop me from passing my exams."

"I do not like to be beaten," said Pheto.

" It is nothing," said Petrus, and suddenly he thought to himself, No, truly it is nothing compared with the happiness of the night in the wagon and the days with the men at the cattle post, the knowledge that I was one of them.

Dineo said to her grandmother, "Will there truly be rain? This evening?" She was looking at the clouds that were gathering now, darkening the western sky where the sun was sinking toward evening.

So often there had been clouds gathering, big, high clouds, flat underneath, sailing over during the day, herds of them, but no drop of rain. Or thunder and lightning playing around the horizon all night, but again nothing.

"This time there will be rain," said her grandmother. "Nthole was over to visit me. He is my friend."

Nthole! The children knew him and were a little frightened of him. He wore very old clothes, so patched you could not tell what their first color had been and he had a little bag made of lion skin and in it were bones, some plain and some with marks on them; there was also a shell and one or two other things, but nobody wanted to look too close. Dineo did not like to think about them. But Nkoko and Nthole always had much to speak about to one another, most of all at the times when they drank beer together. "Did he throw the dollars for you, Nkoko?" Dineo asked in a half whisper.

"He threw the dollars and there was the rain piece pointing at me."

"What else did the bones say, Nkoko?"

"Ah, he threw them for me more than once. We had much talk. He is wise, wiser than all your schoolteachers. Has Letsebe milked the goat yet?"

"I will find you milk, Nkoko." Dineo went to look for it but kept on glancing up at the sky. Sure enough, the lightning was coming nearer. Darkness was building up over the hill, the hill where once there used to be lions, a towering spread of dark brown clouds, for the wind had blown the dust up into the air and the clouds had caught it. And now gusts of wind were coming, sharp and sudden, blowing dust and leaves, pieces of paper, anything that was loose, whipping the trees all one way. Dineo put hot embers into a pot, in case the rain came and put out the fire in the lapa. She stayed with her grandmother in the round hut, but the boys went into the house, only peering out to see how close the cloud was getting.

All around them forks and jags of lightning broke the darkness. They shouted to Dineo to bring porridge. It was not fully cooked but well enough to eat, and she ladled it quickly into the bowls, glancing over her shoulder at the sky. She took them theirs and then took the big pot with the rest of it back for herself and Nkoko.

"There was a dust whirlwind this morning," she said. "Going to school we saw it. We were afraid it would come close, but it kept away."

"Never go near a whirlwind," said Nkoko. "There is a man in the middle with an ax. He could chop off your head."

Dineo was not sure that she believed that, but perhaps it could be so. The dust whirlwinds were frightening, even the little ones. They only came when everything was dry. They could lift all the soil from someone's lands, lift or break the young plants. They made the rain dirty.

And now one could begin to smell the rain. All over Mochudi, people smelled it. It was a mile off still, perhaps more, but the smell was clear and fresh, a touch of coolness about it. Dineo put out some pots and her pail, so that if the rain truly came, they would be filled. The boys put out two or three cans that were in the house.

The lightning streamed in jagged forks, suddenly lighting up the dark backs of the hills. The sun had set behind the clouds and no stars showed. Then came the first drops. The children stood with their hot faces and hands lifted to it and sang, "Rain! make me grow, when will I grow? Rain!"

Two days ago, one of the smaller children who had come to the bore-hole with Dineo, a girl as little as Dikeledi, fell or was perhaps pushed and her pail of water fell on the ground, was spilled and drunk up by the ground, the thirsty earth. The rest of them had all stopped and looked at her, and suddenly Dineo knew

that loss and misery had struck that child, had leapt on her like a leopard. The child did not even cry, but all joy had left her. And now here was water coming down on them all. Why? Why not a month earlier when it would have done so much for all of them?

Coming now, late, it might save a few people's crops or part of them, though the children knew well enough that it would not save their fathers' cattle. It might grow a little grass, enough to put some flesh on the ribs of the poor oxen, give back a little milk to the suckling cows. It began to rain steadily in great heavy streaks of water. They went in and shut the doors. So did most people in Mochudi, though some were still hurrying home, lucky if they had a blanket to put over their heads. "I like the rain at school," said Letsebe. "I like it when it goes drum-drum-drum on the roof and we cannot hear the teacher!

"I wish we had a tin roof here," said Letsebe. "One day our father will put on a tin roof instead of this thatch. Then we shall have much water to drink."

Dineo, in her grandmother's hut, wished that too. To have a tank with a tap and not to have to go to the bore-hole every day! And yet in some ways the thatch was nice. It made a cool roof in summer, much cooler than tin, and a warm roof in the winter. Dineo did not think her grandmother would ever like a tin roof. Nkoko wanted things to be as they had always been, tying the Tribe together, tying herself and her ancestors and her grandchildren. She had looked around the lapa and chosen the corner where she wanted to be buried when her time came. She had told Molemi and Tsholofelo and they had not liked it much, because this is not a modern way of being buried and Chief Linchwe did not want people buried this way. But they also knew that when the time came, they would have to respect Nkoko's wishes.

The rain began to come down harder, as though it wanted to break everything below it. The fire hissed out into black embers. In the house the boys had lighted the lamp, though there was only a little paraffin left in the can and no money for more. But now was the time for it. There was one place above the door where the roof leaked. It needed new thatch, but until the rain came nobody had remembered this. Letsebe opened the door cautiously. In the square of light that came from the lamp they saw the rain streaking down strongly and solidly. The floor of the lapa was glistening with it. "The grass will come," said Letsebe, "the rain will wake up the seeds. The cattle will eat. It is not too late."

"There will be more watermelons," said Pheto, "big ones!" And both of them were hoping that this good rain had come on their father's lands and not only in Mochudi.

Letsebe asked Petrus, "Does it rain like this over in the Republic? Does it rain at your home?"

Petrus was surprised for a moment, because his home

was here. But he thought of his old home and his mother and answered, "Yes, we have rain. People need rain there too for the crops. But mostly they have more rain than here."

"Why do the Afrikaners get more rain?"

"I think," said Petrus, and he remembered his brother saying this, "that they took the countries where there was more rain. They wanted them and they had guns. So now they have good crops almost every year."

"Good crops," said Letsebe, "yes, we have heard that. And where you yourself lived, Petrus?"

"Mostly we have tin roofs and tanks. When a rainstorm came it made a noise so that one could not hear the radio. Even before the rain there was this noise, when the thunder started." And he remembered his brother Joseph and the little old radio set, and how his brother used to sit over it, twiddling the knobs and trying to get news from other places, sometimes even England. Once he had got the set tuned in to Radio Zambia and there had been a storm which made crackling noises in the radio. How his brother longed always for news from the outside, news that would bring hope! And now he was where he could never get it, where hope would be blotted out. Ten years.

Prison. But could one even be sure of that? During the cool morning after the rain he seemed to have more time to be anxious. If his brother died in prison—if he was hurt, killed, and Petrus knew this sometimes happened, or if he killed himself because death was bet-

ter than going on—who would know? Weeks afterwards, an official letter would come to his mother.
They would not tell her at once in case she asked to have
the body for burial; then she might see what had
happened. Suddenly and terribly, in the middle of
school, he felt that his brother must be dead. Joseph was
dead in prison; he had been dead all this time.

The sums he was doing went wrong; he didn't see
where to put the figures. The teacher showed him how
he should have set them down, shook him because he
seemed to be not there, then said, "Are you ill?"
Because Petrus was a good pupil, one who ought to do
the school credit and take a first class in the Primary
Leaving examination. And Petrus gulped and whispered what he thought he knew. The teacher, who
had part of his own family in the Republic, was not too
hard on him. Slowly, the thing passed. Only, his mind
still felt bruised.

It was two weeks later when a message came to Isang
School that Petrus Mangope was to go to the Tribal
Office after lessons. He went in fear—what had happened? Mr. Phirie took him into his little office and
shut the door. Had he done something wrong? Mr.
Phirie set the papers and pencils square in front of him
and looked gravely at Petrus. Then he said, "I have a
message for you from Kgosi Linchwe. From the Chief.
You are to know that your brother Joseph is in the big
prison at Pretoria and he is well."

Petrus began to laugh. It was terrible, this laughter

that took him like a storm. He laid his head on the edge of the desk and laughed, and then he found he was also crying. He looked up and there was Mr. Phirie taking his spectacles off and putting them on again. He said, "The rest of the message tells that your brother now knows you are safe and continuing your education." Now Petrus stared and stared. How had that message gone? It was sometimes possible to send messages to prisoners, but this cost money. What had happened? Who had helped him? "That is all," said Mr. Phirie. "You may go."

CHAPTER 12

From Where Does Strength Come?

FOR A LITTLE IT WAS cooler after the rain. Here and there, grass or herbage came, but it was grazed off quickly. When the children went out to the lands there had been a little rain. It was too late for the corn but perhaps Molemi might get a few beans. Here and there someone with one of the new kinds of quick-ripening corn that was still growing, not yet withered, might get a bag or two. One or two had corners of land with something on them, but the cattle were so hungry that they were apt to break in, even through a strong thorn fence; nothing but barbed wire on strong posts stood up to them if they were not being herded away all the time. And if they got into a field they destroyed it in minutes.

177

Then neighbors were angry, threatened one another, took out their axes and made as if to strike. A man gets angry when he sees his food being taken away. And they all knew that real hunger was not far off.

Prices in the shops were already going up, above all the price of meal, which is the main thing. Sugar was dear too, and some shops had no beans. But meal, meal for porridge: you could not live without that, and if you had no grain of your own, what? Some people were hungry already. There were old women who had no sons working for them. In the old days someone would have taken them on as wives, but nowadays when the Missions said you must have only one wife, that refuge was gone. And they had to go on for many months yet, getting more and more hungry. What was going to happen?

Here and there people were getting work to do, work which would bring in perhaps money, at least food. There were people arranging this for the tribe. There was Mr. Tebape; he was the District Commissioner and his telephone went to the Government, or so Molemi said. And there were those who tried to show people how to grow better crops. There was Mr. Phaloba, the head agricultural officer who had a truck, and the other, smaller agricultural advisers who had bicycles. But not everybody paid attention to what they said. Molemi himself did not listen to them much; they were young men; how could they know as much as he himself knew, he who had been a farmer for more years than they had lived? But Petrus wondered a little at this. Certainly these men were young but they had education, and there were white men also, who had lived long in the country and who seemed truly to want to help the Batswana. There were newcomers too and they were watched and judged by what they did and whether it was done in the right way which fitted in with people's feelings about what was proper. Petrus saw them come to the office and speak with the Chief and then perhaps he would go out with them in one of their trucks, looking for places where dams might be built.

For Chief Linchwe was the leader in this war against hunger, as his fathers had been in other wars with guns and spears. He and Mr. Tebape spoke much together, and there was also the white woman who came to Mochudi every year and had a small, bad car that she drove too fast because she was impatient. Once she had given Petrus a lift in it and he had wanted to speak to her, but he did not know how to begin. They were all of them in this fight against hunger, and there was something called Oxfam which was a big thing. It was from the Oxfam that the maluti meal came, which the schoolchildren and sick people got during the bad times. Perhaps this year the small children might get it too?

One Friday they were back at the lands. The neighbors had killed a goat and had given a piece to

179

them. Another time they would do the same for this neighbor. The little ones had all run to Dineo and she was rocking Maputso in her arms; he did not seem to be as fat and heavy as he used to be. Dikeledi had a sore place on her leg that was not healing; but when Dineo came to mother them they all felt happier. Soon she was pretending to be teacher and making them say letters after her.

She had told Tsholofelo about the shirt she was wearing under the gym tunic, how it got one hole after another and Nkoko could not mend them any longer. And the other dress, the old one, was so torn that she was ashamed of wearing it. But Tsholofelo could not in any way think what to do; perhaps when she came back, she might speak to one of the aunts. For a time she sat beside Dineo with her arm around her, but there was the meat to see to and enough ting in the pot, and this must by no means be allowed to burn. And there was milk, so that altogether there was a good meal for them. Game was very scarce now. But perhaps Molemi might find at least a guinea fowl.

Molemi was talking to the three boys. He said, "I am going to truck that ox. It is all arranged. I have spoken with Norman Molomo."

"The beautiful ox?" said Letsebe. "The one we saw?"

"Yes," said Molemi, "that same ox. I have decided." And Letsebe felt in his bones how hard it must have been to decide to sell that ox, the ox which had meant such pride and beauty. All this was at the back of his father's voice. But a man must be brave.

"Perhaps you will get as much as fifty rands," said Tsholofelo, standing behind the boys. "It is a big ox."

"The Government gives nothing for the hide, nothing for the good liver. They say it all goes to the railway. I shall not get more than forty."

"The railway is rich," said Letsebe, "why should it take our money?"

"It is by taking money that things get rich," said Molemi. He was angry with the railway, but what was to be done? Nothing.

"There is much we need," said Tsholofelo. "There is the place where the rain comes in the thatch above the door in our house at Mochudi. If we had some tin to put under the thatch— There is need for a new kettle; this kettle drips water more and more. Dineo should have another shirt to go with her gym tunic. That thing she has is only holes."

Molemi stood over her and his face was angry. "Kettle!" he said. "Shirt for a girl! I tell you, woman, food. Food will be our need."

"There is almost a whole bag of meal," said Tsholofelo nervously, hushing the little Ketse who had begun to cry.

"Almost a whole bag—and then? I will tell you a thing, my wife. The Chief has made known that he has a friend who is an Afrikaner farmer and this man has offered to let the Chief's people have meal at a fair price, so much less than the shops. I am buying meal, my wife, so that you and all my children shall live."

Tsholofelo murmured something and looked with big eyes at her husband. Dineo whispered to Mosidi to be quiet. It was Petrus who asked, "An Afrikaner! Is this certain, my father?"

"An Afrikaner. He has come over to the Kgatleng and hunted with the Chief. I have even seen him. A young man. Thin."

"But why should he do this?"

"He does it out of friendship. Why not?"

Petrus said uncomfortably, "Can there be friendship between an Afrikaner and—and us? They call us kaffirs. They want only to beat us down, to make us slaves in our own country! Can there be a way of friendship?"

"This one is different," said Molemi. "Perhaps our Chief has made him different. Perhaps when they were out hunting together he saw that the thing his Government says about us is not true. Perhaps the Chief showed him that."

"But they are bad," muttered Petrus, thinking of one thing after another, of how he had been looked at and shouted at, of the prisoners working for farmers without pay, above all of his brother Joseph and the things he had heard spoken by him and his friends.

"It cannot be that all of any nation are bad," said Molemi, "that is not sense. People do bad things because their Government tells them they must. That is all. In their hearts they may be good. Some of them. And now we must drive this ox. You three boys will come with me. Tonight we go to the cattle post. Tomorrow morning early we start to drive."

It seemed that there were five beasts to be driven from the cattle post, Molemi's ox and four others, one belonging to Rapula who was one of his comrades in the same regiment. Sensible people everywhere were selling as many of their oxen as they could get to market, though the slaughterhouse would not take more than it could handle every day. It was certain that if they did not sell, more cattle would die of hunger and thirst. A quarter of the cattle would die all over Bechuanaland perhaps. There was nothing for them to eat now but the leaves of some of the bushes and trees. At the cattle post there were two big bags of biltong made out of one of the oxen which had died. But it was very tough. There had been no fat left anywhere on the ox. Still they ate some with milk that night.

The beasts that were to be sold were driven out of the kraal with shouting and laughter. Everyone had a stick. There was a breeze blowing that was almost cool. You could feel that the worst of the heat was over.

There were three men driving, Molemi, Rapula and another, and half a dozen boys, two of them older than Petrus, boys who would most likely never go to school. But they did not care yet. The men all had guns; they hoped there might be game, something to cook, liver to roast over a fire. "One day," said Letsebe, "I shall have a gun. I know how they work. Twice I have fired my father's gun. I have nearly shot a *phala.*"

"I, too, I shall have a gun," said Pheto and twanged his catapult. But Petrus had never thought of having a gun. It would not have been allowed in the Republic. There, it was an impossible thing for an African to think.

The oxen went along fairly well. Every now and then one would break away but the boys always ran after it shouting, and brought it back. Once when they did that, they found a bush of *letlhapye,* pinky-brown, half-transparent small fruits, a little astringent, but how good a handful of them tasted! The poor beasts tried to graze as they went, snatching a bite here and there, reaching up into a tree for leaves, but they had no chance unless the drivers stopped. They had started as the first light began to creep through the bush and now the sun was high and the shadows small.

Then suddenly there was shouting and a rider coming fast. He yelled at them, "The wild dogs—they are on your track, they are coming, the dogs!"

"Gather the beasts, quick!" shouted Molemi. "Get stones. Turn the beasts to face them! How many cartridges have you, Rapula?"

"Here are two! They are coming, I hear them!"

And all at once, there was the pack of wild dogs racing through the bush straight at them, fiercer than jackals, all jaws and teeth and legs and leaping brindled bodies. The men fired, two rolled over dead, another was wounded, yelping madly, but it barely checked them, and the cattle began to bellow and plunge. Molemi's ox broke to the side with two wild dogs after it. Molemi fired, got one down but the other snapped wickedly at the flank of the ox, held on, the jaws working to crack the bone. And there was the beautiful ox bellowing and kicking, trying to get at the dog with its horns and Petrus and Letsebe running in with stones. "Keep clear!" yelled Molemi and fired again, hitting the wild dog in the body so that it let go, but was struggling up again. And Petrus found himself furiously hammering it with a stone, hammering down on the

snapping jaws, red with the blood of the beautiful ox! And all at once the jaws stopped snapping, the wild dog was dead.

Then it was over, the pack dispersed, the bodies on the ground. Letsebe was driving the ox gently back to the others. The men looked at the bleeding wound, rubbed sand in it, pulled over the skin. Rapula pointed out a tree, the boys ran to it and two of them climbed and threw down leaves, which the others brought to the ox which snuffed at them and finally ate them. "Good, he will do," said Molemi. "We can take them on. But let us go slow in case the wound starts to bleed. Watch it, Letsebe. Petrus, you did well, have you seen the wild dogs before?" Petrus shook his head, "Ah, then that was why you were not afraid! Many men would have been afraid to hammer a wild dog with a stone! But you are a true Mokgatla." They all laughed and Petrus suddenly saw the teeth of the dead dog, fierce, a jaw full of knives, and he was indeed afraid. But fear had kept away from him while he had done the thing that was praised. So all was well.

Molemi cut off the tail of the dead dog and gave it to Petrus. Then they started driving again, carefully. Once they stopped and let the beasts graze, while they lay in the shade. All were thirsty but there was no water; still it was not many more miles. There had been no game sighted. Perhaps the wild dogs had frightened them away, but most likely they had gone far, far, to somewhere with water—far off, perhaps to Ngamiland. People said there was water there always, and it was in Bechuanaland, but cut off by many miles of desert.

Molemi ran his hand over the bite in his ox, hoping the slaughterhouse would not notice, or would think it was something that happened on the journey. And at last they came to the station and there was much more shouting and running, but in the end the beasts were got into the truck. And now indeed Petrus, remembering what had happened, was frightened to his bones. Yet he knew he could do it again. And all was over and he had the wild dog's tail in his hand, and the words of praise from the men warm around him. He was indeed one of them, a Mokgatla. They had said it.

They all walked back on Sunday, carrying the week's food and a piece of the cold goat meat specially for Nkoko. And what did Dineo find? She found that Nkoko had been given a piece of cotton by a friend who worked at one of the stores, and she had shaped it into a shirt to go under the gym tunic. She had done this very well, for it was in blue and white stripes, and these stripes, said Nkoko, would not stay straight, and she did not have a button yet to put at the neck. But it was strong and new and Dineo was happy to have it.

Pheto could not make his sums come out right, and he had to show them on Monday. He wanted to have nice marks put beside the sums. These were very easy sums, adding and taking away, and Petrus got stones and moved them about and showed him how to do the same thing with the figures. When there were real things, Pheto understood. Then he began again to shape his wooden dog, cutting very carefully for its eyes and teeth.

Petrus decided suddenly that he would go down to the community center that evening. In spite of what Nkomeng had said, he had never been inside it. But now he was feeling sure of himself. He knew he could read a book or a newspaper as well as boys older and bigger than he was. He was always praised for his reading at school, sometimes allowed to read ahead of the others. So now he was suddenly determined to go into the reading room of the community center and sit down among them all and show them.

It was a long building. There were big hissing lamps in the hall and the reading room. Sandy the Warden was there talking to two of the teachers from the Secondary School where he himself would go in two or three years. There was Simon with his hair sticking up on end, and his arms full of books, oh yes, he knew them all! What was it Nkomeng had said? You could go into the reading room, just pick up a paper, read! Most of the boys were older than he was, yes, but it didn't matter, he could do anything they could do. He could do more, he was a true Mokgatla. Some of them, he said to himself, are only half Mokgatla. He still had the wild dog's tail in his hand and switched it about. People asked him about it and he told them; it was the best of stories to tell.

He walked boldly into the reading room. There were papers on the table, papers on the shelves, picture papers and papers that had only reading in them. There was a very old typewriter and one of the big girls was very slowly learning to typewrite on it. Most of the boys and girls who were reading were looking through the picture papers, perhaps not really reading much. Petrus thought, I will do better! So he picked up one of the newspapers that had hardly any pictures. It was an old paper, two months old. He spread it on a corner of the table and began to read it, still with one hand holding the wild dog's tail, switching it on the leg of the table.

He had not been reading papers much or thinking about the outside world, or even listening to one of the radio sets that you could sometimes hear in the village, coming from an open door somewhere. So the news in the paper did not strike him as very old. Some of it was about things he did not understand, other countries which he had perhaps heard about, but they were too far to be real. Much was news that would keep anyway, about beauty queens and murders or new plans for beautifying the white part of Johannesburg or speeches by the ones in the Government. And then he saw something that struck his eyes: his own family name, Mangope. He began to read more quickly, past the big words that he didn't quite know. Someone spoke to him across the room, but he took no notice. He did not any longer know where he was.

For there was the meeting and there was the name of his brother, Joseph Mangope, ringleader. But had this meeting, then, been Communism, a threat, a wickedness? Had there been a group of criminals threatening the destruction of the State? As he remembered it, they were only asking for things to be fairer, a little fairer. A little chance and hope for the black man.

And he read about the trial, his brother's name in print, Joseph Mangope, no mistaking it: ten years' imprisonment and eight lashes. So that was what happened to his teacher brother. Not only prison but this other thing. And he knew this was not the caning in Kgotla, when a man is not tied but submits of his own will because he knows he has done wrong. It was this other, shaming and cruel thing, the tying, the laughter, done to a teacher, to a man of dignity and worth. Did they make him cry out? Did they hurt him so much? Oh, he hoped not! A man of uprightness and honor, a man of education. Joseph Mangope.

Petrus sat there under the hissing lamp, the newspaper in front of him, other people all around him reading or talking, but he did not see them. The wild dog's tail dropped, forgotten, out of his loose hand; he was utterly silent, alone. And then his cousin Nkomeng came in. She was one of the girls' choir and she was humming their song. But when she saw Petrus she

190

stopped and looked at him. "What is it?" she said. He pointed to the paper. She read and nodded: "You knew about the imprisonment?"

"Yes, but not—not—"

"Not the lashes?" He choked and nodded. She said, "We knew but it was thought you need not know. Not at once. The Chief said so. You were not strong yet. The thing could have hurt you too much. But now I think you are strong. Indeed strong. I have heard about the wild dog."

And under her eyes he knew that this was true, he knew he had been strengthened. He knew that now he could take this bad news and turn it in his mind into something else. He would be able to write to his mother, who had never put it into a letter, but whose heart must have been bruised by it, and tell her that he too understood. He could perhaps strengthen her. And then he began to wonder if his brother also had some source of strength. He said in a half whisper, "What did *he* think about?"

Nkomeng sat down beside him. "Your brother was strengthened, Petrus. He was strengthened like the martyrs in the stories. They too had cruel things done to them. Petrus, it may be that your brother still suffers, that he gets kicks and blows as well as imprisonment. We know that these things happen. Yes, they happen. Not only to him. But he will be strong to bear them."

"How?" said Petrus, still in a whisper.

191

"He will know that this happens because of Africa. And he will go on believing in Africa. And Africa will strengthen him."

"How?" asked Petrus urgently. "How?"

"In the same way that you yourself are strengthened because now you are a Mokgatla, one of us, one of the Tribe. You know it has helped you." Petrus nodded. "And it will be the same for your brother. Even when he is most alone there in prison, Africa will be with him. Africa is bigger than a family, it is mother and father. Africa is bigger than the Tribe; it is Chief and regiments and doing things together. It is bigger even than our country, than our own Bechuanaland. It is something coming. Africa is so big a thing that your brother is safe."

"My brother is safe," said Petrus. "I think I understand." And he picked up the wild dog's tail from where it had dropped and carefully folded the newspaper and put it away. Nkomeng glanced at him, then went back to where the rest of the girls' choir were beginning their practice, one of them thrumming on a string made tight with a stick on a sounding box. And Petrus thought to himself that beyond the Tribe, beyond hunger and thirst and danger, there was Africa. And it was for this that his brother was suffering. And he must ask for more, more, must find out at school, must himself know this other strengthening. Africa.